PENGUIN
THE OTHER

Peter Benson was born in England in 1956. He was educated in Ramsgate, Canterbury and Exeter and now lives in Dorset. His first novel, *The Levels*, won the 1987 *Guardian* Fiction Prize and a Betty Trask Award. It was described by Jane Gardam as 'a delight – a funny, painful, beautiful book', while John Fowles called it 'as cool and sharp as a glass of cider'. Penguin also publishes *A Lesser Dependency*, his second novel, which was co-winner of the first Encore Award in 1990.

The Other Occupant

Peter Benson

PENGUIN BOOKS

PENGUIN BOOKS

Published by the Penguin Group
Penguin Books Ltd, 27 Wrights Lane, London W8 5TZ, England
Viking Penguin, a division of Penguin Books USA Inc.
375 Hudson Street, New York, New York 10014, USA
Penguin Books Australia Ltd, Ringwood, Victoria, Australia
Penguin Books Canada Ltd, 2801 John Street, Markham, Ontario, Canada L3R 1B4
Penguin Books (NZ) Ltd, 182–190 Wairau Road, Auckland 10, New Zealand

Penguin Books Ltd, Registered Offices: Harmondsworth, Middlesex, England

First published by Macmillan London 1990
Published in Penguin Books 1991
1 3 5 7 9 10 8 6 4 2

Copyright © Peter Benson, 1990
All rights reserved

The moral right of the author has been asserted

Printed in England by Clays Ltd, St Ives plc

Except in the United States of America,
this book is sold subject to the condition
that it shall not, by way of trade or otherwise,
be lent, re-sold, hired out, or otherwise circulated
without the publisher's prior consent in any form of
binding or cover other than that in which it is
published and without a similar condition
including this condition being imposed
on the subsequent purchaser

One

1

I worked on a building site in Battersea, but was accused of sloppy work and got the sack. A man on a hot-dog stand offered me a job. I had to fry the dogs and burgers, and keep buns warm. It was warmer in the stand than on the site, but the view wasn't much.

I began to smell of onions. I was staying with friends who complained about this. I moved in with a labourer from the site, but he only gave me a week. He wasn't tall, but he was heavily built – like a bull terrier. I never had his strength, or the way he moved with a hod.

My mother used to keep a bull terrier called Bruce. She bought him a week after Dad died. She died last year. Her sister – my Aunt Alice – has lived in Brighton since she was eighteen.

Neighbours complained about Bruce when Mum let him into the garden to piss and bark at the trees. One day, he burrowed under the fence and got next door while next-door were at work. They were newly-weds; he wanted to extend the back of the house and landscape the garden. She was very slim and made him concrete an area and sink a pipe in the ground so she could have a rotary clothes line. Bruce sat beneath the sheets, shirts and trousers as they rotated. Inevitably, one of the sheets got wrapped around his neck; Bruce began to turn with the clothes before he stopped and tugged the other way. The sheet came away and he ran back to Mum.

She said, 'Bruce! You bad boy!' The sheet was torn, soiled with earth, a white cotton wedding present from next-door's cousins.

Living on her own with Bruce had made Mum lose her sense of difference. She went upstairs, fetched a blue nylon fitted single sheet and replaced the ruined one with it before next-door got back from work. They were teachers and planning to start a family in five years. Mum bought and cooked better meat for Bruce than she did for herself, so he became strong, fierce and loyal.

One night, someone broke into the stand and stole a packet of frozen dogs and the float. The owner accused me. I proved my innocence by producing witness to my presence in a pub. The owner blamed me. I shrugged and said the stand was his responsibility. The owner fired me, and told me my career in fast food was over. I'd never work a dog stall again, if he had anything to do with it.

I tried to get another job, and another place to live. People told me to forget it so I told them to forget it and went to visit Aunt Alice in Brighton.

I had a vinyl holdall, and caught the last train to Brighton with two minutes to spare. I watched the lights all the way. I had a book in my bag called *The International Seed* (a thriller by Stella Cardini), but I didn't read it.

A woman got on at Reigate. She was going home from a dance, flopped down in a seat away from me, glanced at me once, crossed her legs and closed her eyes.

At Brighton, I walked two miles to Aunt Alice's. It was past midnight when I banged on her door. I had to bang three times before a light came on and I heard her say, 'Who is it?' She was right behind the door.

'Greg,' I said.

'Greg?'

'Your nephew . . .'

'Gregory!' she said, and pulled the chain back, took the latch off and opened the door.

Aunt Alice is a Leninist. She bit a policeman at Greenham Common, and spent twenty-one days in prison at the age of seventy-six. 'Why didn't you call?' she said when she saw me.

'I didn't have time,' I said.

She didn't want me to explain why I was there. We sat in the kitchen and she said I was looking more like my dad.

'Sometimes I feel like him.'

'How could you?'

'I do.'

'Have you eaten?' she said.

'No.' It was half past twelve. She made some toast, fetched a can of beans and said, 'You'll waste away.'

'Yes, Auntie.'

'And don't call me that!'

'Sorry.'

'And don't start apologising!'

I held my hands up, but didn't say anything.

Her hair was tied in a sensible bun. She kept a pencil behind her ear, ready to scribble a thought down on a pad she kept in her pocket. The house was littered with rolled-up balls of paper that bore messages like 'Phone Kenneth', 'Philosophers have only interpreted the world in various ways; the point is to change it', and 'Type minutes.'

*

I didn't do much at Alice's place. It was a tiny bungalow – I slept on her sofa and got in the way. She was patient, and spent her time addressing envelopes to party faithful or writing letters to newspapers.

I didn't know anyone in Brighton – I spent a week roaming the sea front, strolling along the deserted beach and clearing my mind. I could have gone back to London, or to Bristol where I knew people who needed a driver, but I was tired of living on wits. I couldn't help it, but I was tired.

I wanted a quiet life. Alice was writing to the local paper about council housing policy. I was lying on the sofa, eating a biscuit. 'I just want a quiet life,' I said.

'Typical!' she said, and put her pen down. 'Typical! Don't you have any fight?'

'Depends . . .' I said.

'On what?'

'On who pays me.'

She huffed. 'Well, I'm not paying you for anything. You're as bad as your father . . .' She was burning to say something about him, but wouldn't.

'He did his best!' I raised my voice but didn't get up. 'Mum never complained!'

'She never got the chance!'

'Yes, she did!'

'There!' She laughed, and turned away from me. 'You wouldn't stand a chance in a fight, would you?'

'What do you mean?' I swung my legs off the sofa and stood up. I took a deep breath.

'A fight.'

'Want a bet?'

'If I was a fool, maybe I would. Maybe someone like Marjorie . . . She could do with someone like you. You wouldn't go the distance with her.'

'Marjorie?'

Alice nodded. 'Yes. And she'd pay. She could afford to pay...'

'Who is she?'

'Didn't you ever meet her?'

'No.'

'Marjorie...' She picked up her pen. 'She's an old friend. We nursed together, before the war. She was...' Alice looked down at what she'd been writing.

'She was what?'

'A good nurse. She went abroad, came back a few years ago. Look...' She got up, fetched a letter and said, 'It'd be real work. Chopping logs, digging her garden. She was only saying the other day...' She read some of the letter, but didn't show it to me.

'Digging her garden?'

'That's it.'

'Where?'

'Dorset.'

'What?'

'Dorset. You know. It's in a forest, not far from the sea. The fresh air would do you good.'

'There's fresh air in Brighton.'

'She's getting old.'

'I don't know...' I said.

'Do you know anything?'

I shrugged.

'You'll thank her for the opportunity.'

'To do what? Chop logs?'

'That's honest work. Have you ever done any honest work? Do you know anything about that sort of life?'

I didn't think so.

'Digging is as fundamental as you can get,' she said.

'It's in the country?'

'Yes. Bow and arrow country. They eat their babies, all that. Back to basics, Gregory.'

'And fundamental?'

'As you can get. If you want a quiet life, it's the place for you. Quiet as the grave.'

In the morning, I took a train to Waterloo. I had an hour before the Dorset train left, so I sat in a restaurant facing the door and ordered a coffee.

I don't know why I attract people but someone had to sit next to me although there were empty tables all around. 'Wonderful, isn't it?' he said.

'What?'

'They say the train's going to leave at three, then they tell you it's not leaving till half past. Then it's a quarter to four . . .'

I don't understand why people use the wrong words to mean the opposite. Like 'Beautiful weather,' when it's raining, or 'See you soon,' when they will not.

'I said it's wonderful,' the man said. He lit a cigarette and let the match burn until the flame was touching his finger before dropping it into an ashtray.

'I heard.'

'And the fares! Who do they think we are?'

I didn't know.

'And if you're really lucky, you get somewhere to stand!'

I didn't say anything. I finished my coffee and left London at quarter past three.

The Waterloo–Exeter line was run down. I sat in a draughty, rattling train, in a lake of rubbish. Tea came in a cup the size of an ashtray – I didn't bother.

I'm no good in the country. I don't mind a park or trees in the street, but endless fields and woods doing nothing worry me. I'm not just irritated – I feel a heavy, thick dread. I don't like the thought that there's no shop for miles, or that it's miles to the nearest town that never sells anything anyway. I don't know the difference between heifers, steers or bullocks. I like cars passing regularly, and people you don't have to talk to. I don't want to be remembered and then recognised by people I don't know. I never have the right shoes for fields.

I wanted a quiet life, but began to worry that I might be heading for coma. Dad had memories of Kent he used to try and impress me with, but I was never interested. I'm sorry about that now, not because I wanted to listen to what he had to say, but because he wanted someone to hear him talking. Talking about things made them more real to him. Talking over old photographs could make him cry. For a long time, I saw Dad as a strong young man in a photograph, but now all I can remember is him shrunk.

In the year before he died, I got into the habit of taking him for drives to the country, or just around town. It was easier to cope with drivers signing at me for dawdling than it was to keep Dad quiet if I went over thirty, so we caused long tailbacks.

Once I took him to the hop fields of Kent, where he had worked as a boy. He remembered the farmer being generous with food and drink, and the smell of hay. We had to stop near Dunk's Green so he could get out and stick his nose in a barn.

I had to support him as he walked. We had a wheelchair in the boot but he refused to sit in it. As I held him, I smelt the sense of fun and games he'd had with me when I was a child.

We used to play football in the hall. It drove Mum up the wall. We used to play first to ten. He was always the Hammers and would get to nine and then wait for me to catch up, and then let me score and win, but sometimes I beat him square. We had a little rubber ball, and broke the window in the front door five times.

The thin bloke across the road came over once and said, 'You know what?'

'What?' said Dad.

'You want to stick a board over that window. You'll get a hell of a draught blowing in.'

'You want a game?' I said.

The thin bloke smiled, looked over his shoulder; when he looked back the smile had gone. 'I'd better not,' he said, and went back to his house. His wife was called Eve. We didn't see much of them.

I propped Dad against a wall while I opened one of the barn doors. He took shallow, gasping breaths; I never saw him look so shrunk. His nose was like a small prune.

He staggered into the barn and made me lead him to a stack of bales. He stuck his nose right in them and tried to take a deep breath. I stood well back.

Outside, it began to rain, but he didn't notice. An old trailer was parked in the barn, so I sat on it and smoked a cigarette.

'It was like this', he gasped, 'when I was a kid.' His throat made a rattling noise, like supermarket trolleys being pushed into a line down a windy alley.

When I was a kid, I never knew exactly what he did. For a while, he worked in a garage, then it was for the council, then it was for a brewery. Sometimes he'd sign on and paint the house. Mum said he did the best he could for us, and that meant *us*. I was never unhappy, but often felt insecure because our landlord was inhuman. He refused to mend the roof or fix the plaster above my bed. A piece of board was tacked there instead, so I spent five years – of the hour in bed before I slept – staring at the words GRADED EGGS, lit by a screw of light that came over the top of the door from the landing.

When Dad had had enough of the hay barn, I put the cigarette out carefully and led him back to the car. We drove towards Tonbridge. I had my elbow resting on the window ledge. The weather was hot. He swore the old hop fields were outside Whetsted, but they weren't. Someone was building at a crossroads he said he'd waited at with his mother. I never met her. He pointed at an oast house someone was living in. We did find one hop field, but he said it wasn't right, so we drove home.

The train was slow. The fields started quickly after London. Some kids ran up and down the carriages, and foreign students were playing new cassettes on new stereo machines. A man opposite me read a book about the Vietnam war. I wondered about hedges.

One farmer has them for centuries and another grubs them out. Why did the first farmer have them? Why do farmers let single trees grow out of hedges? Why do they make stripes in fields? Why do they leave machines in the rain?

Why don't fields have anything going on in them? For miles and miles through Surrey and Hampshire, thousands of acres were empty. All I saw were a few cows, some sheep and two tractors.

After Salisbury, the train emptied, and the countryside beyond the city seemed denser than before. The fields were smaller, there were more hedges and trees, and big blocks of forest.

There was something hidden out there – I felt safe in the train. I bought a lager from the buffet and drank it standing in the space by one of the carriage doors, with the window closed.

Marjorie met me at Axminster station. The train was three-quarters of an hour late.

The station was a disgrace. Paint was peeling

from the building and the platform was untidy. The staff reflected this decay by saying (when I complained about the late train), 'Yeah. Makes you sick, doesn't it?'

'That all you got?' Marjorie said, interrupting my complaint and pointing at my holdall.

'Yes,' I said.

'Good for you. Nothing like travelling light, is there?'

'I don't think so,' I said, 'no'.

She didn't introduce herself, and had me in her car before she said, 'I knew who you were straight away! Alice phoned. It's wonderful. Thank you!'

'I—'

'She told me all about you!'

'Oh, no,' I said.

'Don't worry. Nothing incriminating. And you look like a good boy.'

She didn't look like anyone I'd met before. The first thing I noticed about her was a tiny blister on her right eye. The second thing was her hair. It was long and snow-white. She wasn't tall (five foot six); the hair blew around at the slightest excuse. She was dressed in army surplus fatigues, all two sizes too big. She didn't wear any jewellery.

'Yes,' she said again. 'A good boy.'

'I'm thirty-three,' I said.

'What does that mean?' she said, and reached across for my safety belt. 'Do it up.'

She smelt of boiled vegetables. Her voice was strong and loud, but not irritating. She knew exactly what she wanted.

'I don't know,' I said.

'I didn't think you would.'

I'd been the only passenger to get off at Axminster. She drove an Alfa. I put her at sixty-five, seventy. I thought I was in an unlikely position, but only because the car was so smooth.

'Nice car,' I said.

'Like it?'

'Yes.'

'Not bad, is it?' she said, and revved up behind a Mini. 'Hear that?'

I nodded.

The engine had a musical note. She patted the steering wheel, and overtook the Mini.

'How is Alice?' she said.

'Fine. She sends her love.'

'I haven't seen her for ages. Has she grown up yet?'

'Grown up? She's eighty!'

'She's a Marxist.'

'Leninist,' I said.

'What's the difference?' She warmed the Alfa for a stretch of dual carriageway. 'Marxist, Leninist. Leninist, Marxist. It's like saying Mickey Mouse isn't a mouse because he wears a dinner jacket.' I leaned towards her. We were doing ninety. We overtook a lorry-load of live chickens. They were poking their heads out of stacked plastic crates, and looked very confused.

Two

2

Dad was in the merchant navy for two years. He joined as soon as he was old enough, and got drunk and made love for the first time in his first port, Naples. The ship was carrying lumber; he always remembered Italy as more than a country. 'A bleeding state of mind, Italy,' he told me once. We were driving slowly through Kent. He would have been alarmed by Marjorie's driving.

'They know how to build a car,' she said.

'You know how to drive.'

'Does that surprise you?'

'No,' I said.

'My father taught me when I was fourteen. Hell of an old bus we used to have.'

She had lived an exciting life, spoken her mind, and lived in different countries. Once she had nursed in West Africa; at a different time she had motor-cycled across Australia, when riding astride was not recommended for women. Aboriginals were amazed. She didn't mind eating bugs with them, or taking all her clothes off for a ceremony. Then, in the night, she was gone. The Aboriginals thought the motorcycle was powered by her thighs, and the headlight shone because she wanted it to.

Her father had owned a shirt factory. Her mother's alcoholism drove her away from home, and then a sense of adventure pushed her abroad. Her father had understood. Secretly he had wished he was her, but he couldn't leave. He had been faithful to his wife, and wished she had had a real interest.

For the last twelve years she had lived in seclusion with three cats, a vegetable garden and the forest that grew all around her. She'd grown too old to travel, and wanted to live in her own house.

Wootton Fitzpaine, Catherston Leweston, Birdsmoorgate and Whitchurch Canonicorum were places on the signposts around Marjorie's. I was born in Grays.

Her place was a lodge, set back from the road, a few miles from the next house. We'd driven into a forest. Trees were dark and solid on both sides, and where there were breaks in them, more trees stood in the distance, rising and falling like enormous waves. I didn't anticipate the turning but suddenly she swerved the car and we swept up a long drive to an oval of gravel in front of the house. 'There we are!' she cried. 'Home! Like the old place?'

I nodded. The dust cleared.

'Old gamekeeper's lodge,' she said.

It looked bigger than it really was, an illusion created by a classical style. Small columns framed the windows, porch and door. The windows were leaded and the walls built of big, pitted blocks of stone. Marjorie leapt out of the car and said, 'I could do with a drink!' but I had to sit there, as if a great pressure was on my shoulders. There was a sudden, deep and unforgiving feeling in the air that blew past the car, stopped to look at me and then blew away.

We sat in her kitchen, in small armchairs. 'I live in here,' she said. 'It's the only room I can keep warm this time of year.' There was a big table, a set of four dining chairs, two big cupboards and a Rayburn. Three cats were asleep beneath it. 'My friend,' she said, and patted the oven door. One of the cats woke up and yawned at her. 'And here's another.' She poured some whisky, passed me a glass, said, 'Sit down,' drank hers and poured another.

'Alice', she said, 'didn't say why she wanted you to stay, but I can guess, if your father's anyone to go by.'

'What do you mean?' I didn't want Dad brought into it. 'She said you needed a hand, so...'

'He never got on with his life.' She drank, held the whisky in her mouth for a moment and then swallowed. 'Mind you, that wasn't necessarily his fault. The male condition.' She turned away. 'You can't help it.'

'What condition?'

She didn't choose to hear me. 'But I suppose I owe Alice something, so we'll do without the explanations.'

'Why do you owe Alice?'

She looked straight at me and said, 'I won't ask you any questions if you don't ask me any. No explanations for no secrets.'

'I—'

'Good,' she said, and when we'd finished our drink she showed me to my room.

It was freezing in there. She had the room over the kitchen, mine was over the front room.

'I didn't get a chance to air it,' she said. It smelt of damp sugar, an old cake tin, dust. I stood at the window and looked out. 'Nice view out there,' she said. 'You've got that.' She patted her hair all over. 'You'll see it in the morning.'

'I can't wait,' I said.

She looked at me. 'Are you being funny?'

'Me?' I said.

The night was solid, but I could see the silhouettes of gently swaying trees. In the distance, the horizon was split into two curves that joined in the middle. Marjorie pointed to some sheets and blankets on a table. 'I put them out,' she said.

'Thanks,' I said.

'You know how to make a bed?'

'Of course.'

'Good. Then when you've done it you can peel me some potatoes.'

'Potatoes?'

'In the kitchen.'

She left me on my own. I shivered. There were pictures around the walls of the room – one of an old woman praying by a window, and another of a cat surrounded by mice. Some of the mice were pulling the cat's whiskers, but it had a scheming look in its eyes, a big bushy tail and strong stocky legs.

We ate late. She told me she'd get me fixed up with boots and a decent jacket in the morning. She had a lot of stuff in a cupboard under the stairs. 'Trousers too,' she said. 'But we'll have to get the boots in town. What size are you?'

'Nine.'

'We'll go to Bridport.'

She had gone to bed and I was sitting on mine when the phone rang. It was half ten. I heard her get out of bed, open her door and walk along the corridor. I put my head around my door.

'What a time to phone,' she said.

'Shall I get it?'

She stopped and looked at me. Her face was inches from mine, and softer than before.

The landing was dark. One of the cats was sitting outside my room. 'Certainly not,' she said, and went down the stairs. When she reached the hall, the phone stopped ringing. 'Typical,' she said. I watched her come back up.

'It might have been Alice,' I said.
'I wouldn't be surprised.'
'Maybe I should phone her and see . . . '
'To Brighton?'
'That's—'
'No one', she said, 'phones Brighton from this house,' and she disappeared into her room. She was wearing a navy blue towelling dressing gown with a red dragon embroidered on the back; like a Hell's Angel, or a Japanese priest.

When I undressed, got into bed and turned the light out, I began to feel my situation.

I couldn't remember ever sleeping in a room that wasn't illuminated in some way – even a crack of light between curtains was enough, but in that room there was nothing but total darkness. Even when my eyes got used to the light I couldn't see anything beyond the faint outline of the bottom of the bed, and the wardrobe and chest of drawers against the opposite wall.

I started the night on my back; spent ten minutes like that and then turned on to my left side. I kept the blankets pulled to my chin. Breathing made my lips cold.

The house was quiet. Marjorie made no squeaks with her bed, the dust gathered in the loft, the Rayburn was damped down and the cats were out. Nothing moved in the freezing front room, or in the hall, on the stairs or outside my room on the landing. Outside, the trees breathed through their leaves and needles.

I turned on to my right side, towards the door. I never get to sleep quickly. I tried to imagine a blackboard. I stood in front of it with a piece of chalk, and the idea is to cover the board with chalk. Usually, you fall asleep before you finish the job. I never have.

Instead, I tried to remember the full names of the

1966 England World Cup squad. I got ten full names, but couldn't remember Cohen's Christian name. I know Geoff Hurst (hat-trick) is in the motor trade now, and one of them is an undertaker. I always said, 'Even if that goal wasn't a goal, we still won the game.' In 1966 we were living in Deptford. We'd bought our first television and invited neighbours to watch the match on it. We were appreciated in our street. I remember looking outside at half-time and the city was deserted, as if people had been hit by a mystery virus that had struck the planet without warning from Outer Space. I was ten.

I strung thoughts and memories, turned over and lay on my back, and slowly felt my eyelids get heavier.

I slept for a few hours before I was suddenly woken up by the sound of a loud cough. A second followed, and then a twenty-second burst. I got out of bed, and thought I'd fetch Marjorie a glass of water at least.

I opened the bedroom door and left the coughing, which started again, behind me. I turned around. It came from outside. I stood with the doorknob in my hand. The milkman.

I went to the window and looked out. The sky was beginning to lighten, and for the first time I could make out some detail of the landscape around the house. I looked down. There was no milkman in the drive.

The house was totally surrounded by trees. Trees disappeared in every direction and as far as the two sloping hills on the horizon. I could see that most had been planted in ranks, but others were in disorganised clumps. Some still had their leaves, others were bare. I couldn't identify any of them.

The sky was the colour of a train window, and looked thin. The cough started up again. It came from the other side of a high wall that ran beyond Marjorie's property. I focused on this, but couldn't see anything moving. Marjorie's garden was a lawn, a few flower-beds, half-dug vegetable plots and a terrace. I could see the corner of a greenhouse and a wheelbarrow parked against a brick shed.

The coughing went on for a few minutes, but I didn't go out to find out who was watching me peek between the curtains. I closed them again, and went back to bed, but didn't sleep.

3

When I was six, I was approached by a man who wanted to touch my private parts. He said he was a doctor, so I asked him, 'Why aren't you in a hospital?'

'I'm a special sort of doctor,' he said. 'I work outdoors, making sure that little boys and girls are being looked after.'

'My mum and dad look after me,' I said.

'Where are they?'

'Home, I suppose.'

'Where's home?'

I pointed down the street. 'Past the shops,' I said.

'Would you like to come in my car and let me show you my home?' he said.

I didn't know. He looked like anyone you might meet in the street. He was wearing a smart brown suit, a shirt and tie, and had a coat over his arm. It was a warm spring day.

I said, 'I'm not meant to go with strangers.'

He said, 'I'm not a stranger.' He smiled.

'Who are you?'

'I told you. I'm a special sort of doctor. And I've got a television . . .'

'A television?'

'Yes. Have you got one?'

I shook my head. No one had a television in our

street. I'd seen one on in a shop, and looked behind it to see the person, but it was magic. It was joined to the person in it by a wire. The special sort of doctor smiled at me when he saw me wondering what to do. He showed me a Mars bar.

'Which is your car?' I said.

'Come and have a look,' he said.

It was a Ford Popular. I touched its headlights. 'How fast does it go?' I said.

'I'll show you', he said, 'if you want. Have you been in a car before?'

'No.'

I was a pretty boy; the only trace I still have is my dimples. I had lots of fine fair hair when I was six. The special sort of doctor ruffled it. I didn't mind. 'Come on,' he said, and opened the door for me.

I got in. The seats were comfortable. He got in too. Before he started it, he put his hand on my knee and squeezed it. I didn't mind him being my friend.

He had put the key in the slot, and was about to turn it when I heard BANG, and saw my dad's face, upside down, looking in the windscreen. He had jumped on to the roof of the car and was staring in at the special sort of doctor. He had a brick. He was fit. The Ford Popular was a very narrow car. He yelled, *'Get out!'* at me.

I got out. Mum was there. She led me away as Dad beat the doctor up. I never watch television without thinking about paedophiles. I don't like Fords. I always lived in cities. I never learnt that you can't trust most people.

Marjorie was up at seven, and got me up at half past. She had breakfast on the table.

'Out your lazy bed!' she called around the door. I was exhausted. The coughing had stopped for an hour, but then started again. It stopped the moment I saw her. 'Tea's hot!'

I sat in the kitchen with my back to the Rayburn, eating muesli. 'Most important meal of the day!' she said. 'Fill the old tank!' She slapped her stomach and grinned keenly.

I nodded.

'You normally this quiet?' she said. She was wearing a red cravat.

'In the mornings.'

'You liven up later?'

'Sometimes . . .'

She poured me a cup of tea, and when one of the cats rubbed her legs, put a saucer of milk on the floor. 'Didn't you sleep well?'

'No. And last night there was this coughing. Did you—'

'Spencer's sheep,' she said. 'I let him put them in the orchard. Did they bother you?'

'It wasn't sheep!'

'Gregory,' Marjorie said, and put some toast on. 'Have you lived in the country before?'

I shook my head.

'It was sheep,' she said. 'I'll show you them later,' and as if to agree, the coughing started again. 'There!' It sounded just like an old man.

Bridport started where a sign said WELCOME TO BRIDPORT, and when I stood at the traffic lights by the town hall, I could look in any direction and see where it finished. I was wearing a German army surplus parka, and Italian army surplus trousers. They still smelt of Marjorie's cupboard under the stairs, but they were warm and I was grateful for that. She dragged me into a shoe shop.

'*Boots!*' she said to an assistant.

I got a black pair, but she didn't make me wear them out. I'd never owned a pair of rubber boots in my life. It was half twelve. 'I need a drink,' I said.

'Good idea,' she said.

I insisted on paying. 'You bought the boots,' I said. 'Do you want something to eat?'

'Why not?'

We ordered mushrooms on toast.

The pub had a low ceiling, brown paintwork, an exposed kitchen and was crowded. While we ate, Marjorie said, 'Spring'll be here before you know it.'

'So what?' I said.

'So I could do with a man about the place.'

I laughed.

She put one hundred pounds on the table and pushed it towards me. I looked at it.

'Go on.'

I put my hand on it.

'It would be a good idea,' she said.

It was the first honest money I'd seen in months. She was the most persuasive old woman I'd met. She said that chopping wood, digging the garden and clearing an area behind the house was worth one hundred pounds.

When the mushrooms came they were the size of beer mats and sprinkled with chopped garlic. I scraped my garlic on to the side of my plate.

'Don't you want it?' she said.

'No.'

She scooped it up with her knife. 'It's the best bit. Good for the circulation too.'

'I don't like the taste.'

'Don't worry about the taste! People always worry about the taste of things, or the look of things! It's what things *do* that matters.'

'Everything does something,' I said.

'Not everything,' she said. I didn't argue.

The hundred pounds sat between us. The toast was saturated with juice. I picked mine up with my fingers. 'OK,' I said.

'Well done!' She beamed. Her eyes were blue. The blister on the right one shone. She showed her teeth when she smiled. They were big and white.

'Just a week though,' I said. 'I can't—'

'A week's fine,' she said. 'You want another?'

'OK.'

She bought a double whisky for both of us. 'Something to celebrate', she said. We chinked glasses and she downed hers in one. It was a Tuesday.

'To us,' I said.

She smiled. 'Us,' she said. 'That's fine.'

There was a huge pile of wood stacked outside the kitchen door. She showed me how to sharpen the axe, and demonstrated the chopping technique.

She put a block on the ground in front of her, balanced a log on it, stood with her legs apart and swung the axe with a relaxed, easy motion. I stood well back.

In the daylight the forest was as open as it could be, given its feel. We were working in a yard behind the house. This was fenced; the trees started twenty yards away, beyond the vegetable garden. They were evergreens, but grey, planted in straight long ranks. When I looked down the ranks, I could feel the silence deepen there so that at the last tree there was absolute, dead silence. I hate not being able to hear cars. I hadn't heard a car since we had got back from Bridport. When Marjorie said, 'Are you going to stand there all day or work for your living?' I thought about Dad.

'No,' I said.

She gave me the axe.

I spat on my hands, straightened a log on the block,

aimed, swung and missed. She laughed. 'You'll get the hang of it,' she said. 'Do that lot and maybe I'll get the kettle on.'

'All of them?'

'It's called work.'

The pile was enormous. I chopped until I couldn't hold the axe any more. I got blisters at the roots of all my fingers. I noticed Marjorie had been watching from the kitchen window with her face like a moon. She opened the window and called, 'That'll do, Gregory. Come and have a cup of tea. I'll show you the wheelbarrow later.'

'Wheelbarrow?'

'Yes. I want them stored before supper time. And it's getting dark. Come on.'

I should have bought some gloves in Bridport but wouldn't complain. Dad never got on with his life, but he never complained, and taught me to work when you're paid. I don't want to cheat anyone. I've never committed a crime. I could have, but I need to be honest. I just can't see myself past go.

I was hopeless at school, and easily led. I was the one who didn't mind doing the dirty work for the ones who'd done the planning, like stealing confiscated items back from a teacher's desk, or putting glue on the globe. I failed. I was beaten. I never had ambition. While boys and girls around me decided to become gas fitters, nurses, air traffic controllers and joiners, I developed a vacant look. I kept this on my face for the last two years of school and the first year after it. I was a walking badge.

Sometimes I did labouring – mixing cement, shifting bricks – mostly I signed on. Dad supported me. Mum didn't complain. She'd had twenty-five years to get used to Dad, and had been expecting it with me. In some ways she looked forward to seeing it happen, so she could be reminded of her courting days.

I barrowed all the logs to a shed – it was dark by the time I finished.

Marjorie had no outside light. The night was pitch, and very cold. As I stacked the last logs, I heard a distant cry like a child's. It hung in the air for a moment, and then was carried away.

I left the shed and stood in the yard. I stared at the sky. A single star was shining directly above me. The cry came again, but twice this time, through the trees to where I stood, like a breath.

I wasn't going to be fooled again, so I walked towards the noise. I crossed the vegetable garden and stood by a fence at the edge of the forest.

Although there were no trees behind me, as I stood with trees in front of me it felt as though they gathered me in and I was surrounded on all sides. The tops rustled in the wind, but the air in front of me was still. I hopped over the fence – the cry came again. This time, it was closer – somewhere to my left.

I stood absolutely still. Suddenly, a rushing sound came from the branches above me – I turned. The lodge seemed further away than it should have been. I got a prickling on my neck, and then a rush of blood that travelled from my feet to my head in a second. The rushing stopped and the cry came again, directly above me, like it was at me, or hated me.

I ran and heard it once more before I stumbled towards the kitchen door.

'Marjorie! Quick!' I dragged her outside. Her arms

were covered in flour, but I made her listen. It came again, closer this time. 'There! Hear it?'

One of the cats joined us on the doorstep. It looked at me as if I was less than a plant.

'Owls,' Marjorie said. 'Protected species, owls.'

4

After supper Marjorie let me off washing up, and when she'd done it said, 'I'll buy you a drink.'

We went to the pub.

We drove for twenty minutes through the narrowest and most winding lanes I'd ever seen; over hills, down again, through woods, around blind bends and across tiny crossroads. I knew that if I was outside the car, walking home, I'd never find my way, but I felt safe. The Alfa was a dream. The heater was quiet, and warmed the car quickly. I relaxed, and when I reached out and turned the radio on, Marjorie didn't mind listening to rock 'n' roll.

The pub was run by a man who didn't bother to serve us straight away. No one talked to us.

The other customers were farmers; the buzz of conversation quietened when we walked in. I had a pint of lager, she had a whisky. We sat by the door, with a view of the bar. There was a notice on the wall about a fun run, and a piece of green tinsel hanging from a corner of the ceiling.

The farmers got used to us, and carried on drinking. Some played darts, but mostly they huddled in a group and pointed at each other as they talked.

'They don't like you,' I said to Marjorie.

She nodded, and poked at her hair. A piece of it

stuck out like a finger. 'They don't like a woman on her own. I make them nervous.'

'Why?'

She scratched her face. 'Are you always this stupid?'

'No.'

'So you admit—'

'No! I don't! I meant that I'm never—'

'Stupid? That's a rare accomplishment!'

'No!' I shouted.

The farmers looked up. I looked at them and waved my hand. Marjorie smiled.

'We're meant to be looked after,' she said. The farmers looked away. 'They don't like the idea that a woman can look after herself. It makes them think they might be dispensable.'

'Isn't everyone?'

'Of course. They think I'm going to steal their wives or something. But they can think what they like. I'm the local witch,' she said, and smiled.

It wasn't the smile of a witch.

'You're not,' I said.

'Once', she said, pointing, 'I came in here wearing a German surplus shirt. It had ENGEL printed on the front, and little German flags sewn on the shoulders,'

'I know them.'

'Warm. Cheap too, but I got this abuse about the war!' She laughed again. Her laugh disturbed the farmers. It wasn't manic but it was loud and loaded with direction. 'I told them about the Common Market.' She raised her voice. 'They don't mind the subsidies, but nothing much changes around here. They still eat babies . . . ' She finished her whisky and fetched another and a lager for me.

She was telling me about the next day's work (pruning) when a car revved into the car-park, doors banged shut, young people laughed and shouted. There were three of them, and they tried to get through the pub door at the same time.

'Look out,' said Marjorie.

'Why?'

'You'll see.'

The woman was Sadie, the bigger bloke was her boyfriend – Nicky – the other bloke was Jack. Jack was small and agreed with everything Nicky said. Nicky was taller than Sadie.

Sadie had long wavy brown hair and a slim, pale face. Her nose, eyes and mouth were small. When she smiled, she showed a dimple in her right cheek. Her lips were thin, but when she opened her mouth they seemed to grow, like a flower opening. I heard her say, 'A dry Martini.' Her voice was like a stage whisper. I wanted to spend at least two weeks with her.

Marjorie noticed my look. She shook her head and said, 'Don't even think about it.'

'Why not?' I said. The lager was warm.

'He's a big boy . . . ' she pointed at Nicky, 'and he's not too clever . . . '

'She looks bored,' I said.

'Well spotted. But maybe he's a good lay.'

'Marjorie!' I said.

'What's the matter? Don't you want me to speak my mind? Afraid of a bit of truth?'

'Saying that maybe Nicky's a good lay isn't the truth.'

'Granted. But that doesn't stop me speculating.'

'Do you speculate like that about everyone?'

'No.'

'It's . . . ' I said.

Marjorie leant towards me. The whisky had given her a mellow, abandoned look. 'Don't you like the idea of an eighty-two-year-old woman with a dirty mind? Too much for you?'

'Eighty-two?'

'Yes. That's the other thing they don't like.' She waved at the customers.

'You're not eighty-two!'

'Don't give me that.'

'But you look—'

'I know. Remarkable, isn't it?'

She didn't have to be facetious with me. 'Yes,' I said. She believed me. 'It is.'

Nicky noticed us, but didn't move. He was mean-looking with broad shoulders, fat hands and a paunch. Jack had a nervous twitch; he looked at me quickly, then looked away, as if I wasn't worth it and he hadn't looked in the first place. He had long greasy hair, and a shadow of hair on his top lip. Sadie carried on looking beautiful. All the farmers gave her sly glances, and then leered at each other. She held her arms across her chest. She looked at me.

I'd had a bath before coming out, and washed my hair. My army surplus clothes gave me a dangerous, angry air; sitting with a witch gave me some mystery. More important, I'd shaved. This gave my face a bone-white sheen. My pores were closed.

I smiled at Sadie. She sipped her drink and then ran her fingers through her hair. Her eyes widened for a moment, and I thought she made a move towards me, but she turned back to Nicky and I heard him say – about his car (a Capri) – 'It's got Macpherson struts. Smooth as silk. It's a bloody miracle.'

5

The sheep coughed again that night, and were joined by the wind as it whined through the forest. Marjorie had lent me an *Observer's Book of Trees*.

'Those are sitkas,' she'd pointed out. 'But there are Scots pine, larches and birches too.'

All the trees looked roughly the same to me, but I wanted to educate myself while I was there. I read in bed.

'Bristle cone pines in the Arizona deserts live as much as 4000 years . . .'

' . . . this process, called photosynthesis, can only occur with the aid of the marvellous chemical substance called chlorophyll.'

The book was perfect for carrying in the pocket.

When I'd read about sitka spruces 'every needle has a sharp point. This makes sitka unacceptable as a Christmas tree', I turned the light out and waited for a thought to occupy me for an hour before I fell asleep.

I sneaked off to walk in the forest with the *Book of Trees*. I'd spent the morning cutting dead wood out of apple trees in the orchard. The sheep stood and watched me, but were very nervous. I tried to soothe them by talking, but they didn't listen.

I hopped over the fence that bordered the far edge of the orchard, and followed a line of trees until I reached a track. I followed this down a hill and found myself in a hollow.

The ground was soft and springy, the peace framed by the gentle swish of the trees' top branches. One or two birds screeched alarmingly; I walked out of the hollow. The track narrowed and passed through a rough coppice.

Beyond this, a small area of cleared ground had been planted with saplings. Each was marked with a white stick, and protected by a plastic bag. Suddenly, two RAF jet fighters appeared from nowhere and swung across the horizon, dipping their wings and dropping quick dark shadows across the plantation. Then they were gone and I was alone again. I turned back into the forest.

I headed towards a hill planted with taller, greener trees than the rest. They were easy to identify as Scots pine. 'A reliable tree'. As I headed back the way I'd come, but taking a different route when I reached the turning back to Marjorie's, I enjoyed the tangy air, and picked up a pine cone. It was fresh. I put it in my pocket.

I got a good sense of smell from my dad. He never said he wanted to live anywhere but town, yet he loved the country for the memories it had given him. Mum had a green vision of England too, connected to an idea of plenty of food – eggs, milk, cheese, fresh meat and home-made bread. She could do wonders with a pint of water, three turnips and an onion, and cultivated a window-box until cats got at it.

I was sitting beneath one of the Scots pines, watching a lane a mile away. There was a farm between the trees and the lane. Some sheep were grazing the field beyond the edge of the forest. Someone came from the farm, whistled for a dog and began to head towards the sheep. The sun was setting.

The trees faded as the light faded, so those I could focus on two hundred yards away began to blur and then merge into closer ones. The brightest patches of sky turned pink. I stood up and began to walk back the way I'd come.

I'd been going for ten minutes when I realised I was lost. I found myself on a path bordered by tall shrubs with glossy green leaves. It was muddy and after a few turns in the path I couldn't work out if I was heading in the right direction. The ground rose and I walked into a small grove of scrubby trees.

I was trying to be sensible and keep calm when I heard a dog barking behind me. The light was fading very quickly; I retraced my steps, hurrying through the glossy shrubs. My rubber boots kept my feet dry, but my legs were tired. Suddenly the dog appeared and was rushing me when a voice yelled, 'Rusty!'

The dog stopped in its tracks but didn't take its eyes off me. It lay down and guarded me like a sheep until Sadie came around the corner and said, 'Stay!'

'All right?' I said, calmly.

'Yeah. You?'

'I was. I'm a bit lost though, I think.'

'A bit?'

'Only in this wood. I'm OK otherwise.'

She thought that was funny. She was fascinated to learn that Marjorie had someone helping her. 'No one from round here would go anywhere near her.'

'Why not?'

She shrugged. 'I don't know. I don't mind her. Everyone needs a bogeyman.'

'She's not mine.'

'Nor mine.'

She wasn't spooked by the darkening forest or me; I kept close to her. I didn't like the feel of the trees but liked the sound of her footsteps on the needles on the path. When it was wide enough for us to walk side by side we did.

She remembered me from the pub. When I asked her about her boyfriend Nicky she said, 'I suppose you could call him that. I've known him all my life. He likes to think he owns me already.'

'Already?'

'Everyone says we're the perfect couple.'

'Who's everyone?' I said.

She didn't say anything, but looked sadly at the ground.

Why was Sadie confiding in me? I have an open, honest face. She had confidence in the woods, but I didn't get mine back until we reached the road. I didn't recognise it. 'You're just down there,' she said, pointing. She had slim, delicate fingers.

We walked another half-mile before we reached the lodge. We watched Marjorie through an uncurtained window. She said, 'I've got to get back.' She had milking to do, calves to feed and bales of hay to carry to a barn in a field of sheep.

'I'll see you again,' I said.

'Maybe,' she said, meaning 'Good'. I could see it in her eyes.

'Maybe?'

'I don't get much time off.'

'Make time.'

'Make time . . . ' she said.

'Yes. Treat yourself . . . '

We were standing a couple of feet apart. 'Treat myself?' She moved towards me, reached out and touched my hair. 'You need a trim.'

'No, I don't.'

She looked at it. 'You've got a streak of red in it.'

I reached up and touched her hand. 'It's always been like that,' I said.

39

She laughed. Rusty barked and jumped up at her. She stepped back and brushed her clothes down. 'He gets jealous,' she said.

'I'm not surprised.'

'He's a good dog though, aren't you?' She patted his head, like she'd done with me.

'My mum had a bull terrier.'

'They're all right.'

As she walked away, I thought she looked bored, and that there was nothing worse than feeling trapped. Since leaving school, she'd worked on her parents' farm. She had green eyes. Marjorie opened the window and called, 'Gregory?'

'Hello, Marjorie!'

After supper, I did the washing-up and confirmed to her that she was a witch. 'Sadie told me no one round here would go anywhere near you. You scare them.'

'Them?'

'Yes.'

She laughed and told me to be careful with Sadie. A boy she'd really liked had been beaten up by Nicky and Jack.

'Sod them,' I said.

'They know all about sodomy.' She stoked the Rayburn. 'Buggery, sodomy,' she said. 'They went to private schools.' She told me which ones. They were in the West Country.

I told Marjorie the name of my school. She told me the name of hers, and for a while, reminisced about it.

6

When I was at school I was kicked in by a boy (Derek) who thought I'd kissed Sandra Wilkins the librarian's daughter. She had red hair and big lips. She lived away from the estate, but the librarian voted Labour and insisted that they live like everyone else (except in a bigger house).

Sandra had seen books you had to ask for in writing if you wanted to borrow them; she passed me a note in class. It read, 'I've got the book. Meet me after. Love Sandra.'

The book was called *Love and Teenagers*.

After we'd read enough she said, 'Give me six-pence and I'll show you my knickers.' She hitched up her skirt and showed me her knees for nothing. They had little spots of blood on them.

'I haven't got sixpence,' I said.

'Oh,' she said.

'I've got thruppence.'

'Is that all? Thruppence?'

'Yes.'

I watched her think about it for a while before she decided to show them to me for thruppence.

She lifted her skirt as Derek lurched around the corner and caught us. He'd seen Sandra's bottom, and was upset to see me there. I was eight, he was ten. I lived in a terrace, he lived in a semi, Sandra lived in a detached. She had fat thighs. He had big fists. I got a black eye. I told Mum I'd fallen over in the classroom and banged against a desk. Dad agreed that it was a shiner; I wore it like a badge. Sandra, proud that I had been hurt for her, told her friends I was a hero, took her clothes off for me, and said Derek had a prick no bigger than a fag end.

Colonel Hilary Franklyn drove a twenty-eight-year-old black Rover 95. He parked it in front of the lodge and when the smoke had cleared, climbed out. He spotted me immediately. I was mending a fence, but stopped to say hello. He said, 'At ease.'

'Morning,' I said.

He walked with a stick. He had an acute limp, a red nose, a pipe in his mouth and a bald head.

'You'll be the chap who's mucking in with Marjorie.' He took his pipe out and pointed at the fence with it. 'It's high time someone straightened the old place out.'

'Yes,' I said.

'You look just the ticket.'

'I'm—'

'Good show!' He patted me on the shoulder, said, 'Carry on,' patted his chest and went to see Marjorie.

I joined them an hour later. They were playing cards on the kitchen table, but didn't offer to deal me in. I had a cup of tea instead. They'd opened a bottle of whisky.

Marjorie laid her cards down and introduced us. The Colonel was down twenty matches, and not in the mood for small talk, but this was normal. 'She's giving me a run for my money,' he said.

'If it was money,' she said, 'I would be giving you a run. But matches . . .' She waved at them. 'I'm just fooling, really. Playing.'

'See what I mean?' The Colonel looked at me. 'She's playing with me! She thinks I'm a child!'

She smiled, fiddling with some matches.

I wasn't any help, so I drank my tea and left them to it.

Marjorie had given me a special tool for stretching wire tight, but it was rusted. I improvised with an iron bar, and made sure that all the posts were upright. The weather was cloudy, with sunny intervals. When I hammered the staples, the noise echoed through the forest and startled some birds that had been watching.

I finished the job, and enjoyed it, but by lunchtime I needed a fix of traffic and pedestrians. The Colonel had left – cleaned out of Vestas. In forty-eight hours he'd been only the third person I'd seen. I was beginning to hear silence as a faint buzz in my ears. I complained about it to Marjorie as we ate vegetable soup, warm bread and cheese. She said 'We'll go to Lyme. I've got to do some shopping.'

We parked, and while Marjorie looked at the sea and took deep breaths, I admired the car-park and the shops. Some of these were shut although full of holiday souvenirs. A couple of faded pennants advertising ice-cream fluttered in the wind.

Lyme was a modern town with some old houses tacked on the front and sides. These houses, and the old walls of the harbour, rebuked the rest. The town had history if it made money. Signs on telegraph poles warned dog owners to look out.

Marjorie shopped while I sat on a wall in the main street and watched traffic jam. I enjoyed the smell of petrol fumes, and the busy people as they walked up and down. I bought a local paper and sat on a wall to read. The hot story of the week was ANGER OVER PRIME FREE TRADE SPOT.

The town clerk had been offered prime sea-front premises, rent free. He was planning to set up a shop. The premises were owned by the town council. The decision to let the clerk set up this shop had been taken at a closed committee meeting.

The town mayor had said it was in the public interest that the decision was made behind closed doors. 'The matter was thoroughly debated, points were raised and discussed and the decision was upheld,' he said. 'He's a first-class town clerk,' he concluded.

Local traders had been campaigning unsuccessfully for years for permission to trade on the sea front. Another story was about Valentine's Day. Romance was not out of fashion in Lyme.

I went to a café for a coffee. From my seat I could see some men repairing the masonry around a flight of steps that led from the raised pavement to the road. When Marjorie joined me I said, 'I can't get used to these little places. But I'd like to . . .'

'Good for you!'

'Everyone knows everyone else, don't they? You couldn't get away with anything.'

'Nothing,' she said, and she ordered a Danish. When it came, it had a small sweet cherry on the top. She put this on the side of her plate and ate the pastry first. It had mashed apple inside.

I drank some coffee and asked about the Colonel.

'What's to tell?' she said. 'He comes round, we play cards, he loses and goes home. He's very formal.'

'Military.'

'I wasn't going to say that. He never talks about it – I think his work was all a bit hush-hush.'

The coffee was hot.

She said, 'They used to call them gentlemen, I think.' She popped the cherry in her mouth, chewed it and wiped the corners of her mouth and her fingers on a paper napkin. 'A man's got to have a sense of humour. Hilary's a bit stiff.'

'A bit stiff?' I laughed.

'Yes,' she said, refusing even to smile. 'He used to live with his mother. She only died a couple of years ago.'

'She must have been ancient!'

'Getting on . . . ' She laughed.

'What's funny?'

'He had a lift put in the house so she didn't have to climb the stairs. She was very frail. It was a proper lift, like in a hotel. The real thing. He always insists on the best.'

'So?'

'So she didn't mind using it, but was worried about getting stuck between the floors. So he bought a lumberjack's axe and hung it—'

'In the lift?'

'Yes!' She slapped her thigh and roared with laughter. 'I always imagined her in there, swinging at the doors with that axe. Steel doors – she could hardly lift a dinner knife!'

I laughed.

'I don't think Hilary thought that one through.'

I was thinking about having a Danish but she finished hers, stood up, whacked me on the head with her gloves, said, 'Come on!' and left a tip.

We walked back to the car slowly; she took my arm.

'Good shops in Lyme,' she said.

'Are they?'

'Yes. You'd be surprised.' She showed me a goat's cheese she'd bought, and some fresh fish.

'I've never had goat's cheese before,' I said, smelling it. It smelt of piss.

'I think it's good for the circulation.'

'Which circulation?'

'You know what I mean.'

There were some hippies sitting on a greasy slope near the car-park. They were eating sandwiches and laughing about something. An old bloke with a beard was putting bottles in a bottle bank. Some of the gardens of the houses around the car-park were tidy and attended. Marjorie made me stop for a moment so that she could catch her breath. 'I'm sorry,' she said. 'It's not like me.'

'Do you want to sit?' I took her arm and pointed to a bench. She shrugged me off.

'No!' She looked angry.

'Just take your time then,' I said.

'There's not enough of that.'

'What do you mean?'

'I mean . . .' she said, but didn't finish what she was going to say. She walked past me to the car.

There was a sign to a footpath that ran along the coast in either direction. Some serious walkers were heading through the car-park. 'They've butchered those,' Marjorie said.

'What?'

'The cedars.' She pointed to some enormous trees beside the road. 'Butcher anything.'

The bungalow and house gardens we passed on our way home were neat and private. Marjorie drove fast; I kept my brake foot pressed to the floor. She noticed this and said, 'I'll brake. You relax.'

'I am,' I said.

The Alfa Romeo 164 3.0 V6 cost £17,925.00. For an extra £2325 she could have had air-conditioning, alloy wheels, a sunroof and a CD player. Marjorie didn't have any CDs. An underdoor light came on when the door was opened and lit up the road to make entering and getting out of the car easier in badly lit areas.

We accelerated from 0 to 60 in $7^1/_2$ seconds, taking a different route home. Instead of turning into the forest where I expected she drove on, past Lambert's Castle and through Marshwood.

At Birdsmoorgate, she stopped in a lay-by beside a cottage, and rested for a moment to admire the view that folded out below us. The fields were bright green, dotted with trees and clumps of woodland. To the right, the forest stretched along a ridge as far as the eye could see – in the distance I could see the sea between two hills. It was quiet there. The garden of the cottage we were parked next to was well tended.

'There aren't many places like this,' Marjorie said.

'Like what?'

She looked at me. 'Are you serious?' she said, and when I didn't reply, looked away again.

7

Mum didn't like cars. The only time I ever got her into one with no trouble was when we bought Bruce from Battersea Dogs' Home. She dressed for the occasion, in a blue dress she'd last worn to a wedding and a green hat. She looked ridiculous but dignified. I held the passenger door open for her, so that she could step into the car with ease, like the Queen.

'How far is it?' she kept saying.

'Only a couple of miles. Half an hour.' We were sitting in a traffic jam.

'We could have walked it.'

I said, 'Enjoy the view,' and pointed to the river.

Bruce waited for us in a cage. He didn't bark or wag his tail and pant when we stood in front of him. He had two empty bowls and a bed.

'He's an example to us all,' Mum said, when she saw him. The official nodded and said, 'He's a dear, isn't he?'

'Yes.'

'He's called Bruce.'

'Bruce?'

'Yes.'

'It suits him.'

I kept out of it.

Bruce enjoyed the drive home. He and Mum formed an instant bond. He knew exactly who she was and what was required of him. He looked at me suspiciously, and bared his teeth. Mum said, 'No! That's Gregory,' so he sat back and rested his head in her lap while she stroked his jowls and ears.

I was going to say that I could stay longer than a week when Marjorie had an accident. I was outside with a spade. She'd demonstrated the correct way to dig a vegetable garden. You make a trench and fill it with earth from a second trench, weeding as you go. Birds came from the forest and lined up along a fence to watch. One came as close as the wheelbarrow, and dived for worms.

'I don't know why I bother,' she said. 'Nothing grows, but I've got to try. I feel guilty if I don't.'

'Guilty?'

'Yes,' she said. She coughed. 'Have you ever been to China?'

'No.'

'If you had, you'd know what I mean.'

'What *do* you mean?'

'If they can hoe it they'll cultivate it. There's a lot of mouths to feed in China.'

'But this isn't China.'

'But it's the idea,' she said. 'You've got to act good sense, even if you don't think it all the time.'

'If you say so,' I said.

'No! That's the whole point! Not if *I* say so. It's got to come from you!'

'Right,' I said.

'Right?' she mumbled. 'Right? What right?'

I didn't know.

She didn't insist on knowing.

The trees shaded the garden for all but a few hours in the middle of the day, and pine needles were no good as a mulch, but she said, 'It's got to come from you,' again, before handing me the spade and going indoors to roll some pastry. Two of the cats sat on the doorstep and watched me; the other was hunting in the woods.

I'd been working for ten minutes when I heard a cry from the house and the noise of a chair going over. I dropped the spade and ran to find Marjorie lying on the kitchen floor. She said, 'Bloody hell.'

'What happened?' I said.

'I got old.' She tried to move. *'Ouch!'* she yelled.

'Have you hurt yourself?'

She gave me a withering look. She held her arm. 'I think I've broken it.'

'That bad?'

'Yes,' she said. 'And it gets worse.'

'How?'

She paused, with her mouth open, ready to say something.

'How?' I said again.

'You'll have to drive me in.'

This wasn't what she meant to say, but it had to do. Whatever she wanted to hide was showing.

'Where?'

'Dorchester, I suppose.'

'In the Alfa?'

'What else?' She smiled. 'Your dream come true?'

I couldn't disguise my pleasure. 'One of them.'

She made me wash my hands and change my trousers before I drove. She sat in the passenger seat and moaned about adventuring round the world and never a slip, but rolling pastry and look at me now. She thought she was stupid, but I disagreed.

'Most people die in bed,' I said. 'So that must be the most dangerous place you can—'

'Gregory?' she interrupted.

'Yes?'

'If you're going to say anything, make it sensible.'

When we got to Outpatients, she refused to believe the doctor was qualified. He was very thin.

'I assure you that I am,' he wheezed. He had a plasticised name tag to prove it.

'You could have got that anywhere,' Marjorie said.

'That's true,' he said, 'but I didn't.'

He was patient, even though he had been working hard. He called me Marjorie's son. She laughed. I winced. He called a nurse and told her to arrange for Marjorie to be X-rayed.

Marjorie was grateful for my presence, but refused to let me accompany her to X-ray. I sat in the waiting room and watched a sculptor.

Dorchester Hospital was a new building, and decorated with bright blue and red window frames, gables, pipes and wooden slats. The different wings met around courtyards – the sculptor was working in the biggest of these. He was carving a fountain and waterfalls out of blocks of rock. He was covered from head to foot in dust. There was a shop run by volunteers in the waiting area, and some countryside and house magazines.

The sculptor was having trouble with an electric grinder when the doctor came back and said, 'She's broken her arm in two places.' He yawned. 'Very brittle, old people.'

'She'll be all right?'

'Oh, yes. Of course. She's a fighter, but I think, as a precaution, we'll keep her in for a couple of days.'

'Keep her in?'

'Yes.'

'She won't like that.'

'She doesn't. But sometimes in cases like these, there can be an element of delayed shock. We'll be running a few checks while she's here.'

'Shock?' I said. 'I don't think you could shock Marjorie.'

'All the same.'

An undernourished nurse took me to Marjorie's room. The hospital was like a hotel. There were exhibitions of paintings and photographs on the walls, and the wards were divided into small rooms. I had never seen Marjorie in bed before. 'Look at me!' she cried, when she saw me. 'And they want me to stay in!'

Her arm was plastered. She was wearing a hospital nightie. I offered to fetch her one of her own, but (1) she wasn't having me rummaging through her things, and (2) I wasn't driving the Alfa more than I had to.

There were two other women in the room. One was asleep. The other was reading a newspaper.

A doctor came and told Marjorie that she could leave the following afternoon. I told her I didn't mind staying on at the lodge for as long as she took to mend. 'Thank you, Gregory,' she said.

'I've nowhere else I've got to be.'

'It's still good of you,' she said, and she gave me a list of things that had to be done.

I left her breaking the ice with her companions by saying, 'I could do with a drink. Anybody got some whisky?' The sleeping one didn't stir; the other shook her head and went back to her paper. Marjorie couldn't cross her arms, so she fiddled with the hospital radio and headphones, until a nurse came and sorted them out for her.

I felt as if I was in a dream as I drove back to the lodge. The road from Dorchester was switchbacked and straight; every now and again a glimpse of the sea appeared between dips in the hills. There were vast stretching views of the fields and hills inland and as the sinking sun coloured everything gold, for the first time in my life I wasn't worried by the countryside, or by the thought that the car I was driving would break down. Sheep moved across the fields like lights. I cruised at seventy. The instruments were unfussy, the engine was as smooth as silk and the gearbox just stiff enough. The seat was adjustable. I'd told Marjorie I'd be careful.

I got back to the lodge as the sun was setting, wiped my feet, put the kettle on and studied Marjorie's list.

Keep Rayburn in
Finish digging
Feed cats ($^1/_2$ tin each plus biscuits)
Chop and stack wood
Phone Colonel Franklyn

I made a pot of tea, memorised the list and fed the cats.

On my own in the old gamekeeper's lodge, with the Alfa parked outside, I could imagine myself as the boss. Marjorie didn't have a television, so I was listening to the radio and reading another book about trees when someone knocked on the door. It was half past eight, dark outside.

I hadn't heard a car in the drive, or footsteps on the gravel. By the time I reached the front door, I had counted all the people it could have been.

Three.

It was Sadie. The first thing she said was, 'I've never got this far before.' The light was fading but I could see her face clearly. She didn't have any spots.

'What?'

'Up to the front door.' She peered in. 'It is a bit creepy, isn't it?'

I shrugged. 'You get used to it.'

She edged towards me. 'When we were kids we used to dare each other to knock on this door.'

I couldn't imagine her as a kid. She asked me if I wanted to come for a drink. I explained about Marjorie's accident, and said, 'I can't leave the place.

I promised I'd keep an eye on things, but there's some beer in the fridge. Do you want to come in?'

'Do you think I should?'

'Who's watching?' I said.

She looked over her shoulder at the forest. At night, it seemed to come closer to the lodge. The trees grew together, so they made a solid wall of gloom that grew out of the sky's darkness. I didn't notice any clouds, but couldn't see any stars either.

'I don't know,' she said, nervously. 'You never know...'

'Come on,' I said. 'You'll get cold.'

'OK.'

We sat by the Rayburn and drank out of cans. She loved cats. We talked about satellite TV, the ozone layer, trees and farming. She didn't want to work anywhere else but on a farm, but wished she had more time to herself.

'Where's Nicky tonight?' I said.

'Up the pub. I was meeting him there.'

'Does he know you're here?'

'No.'

'And you were going to turn up with me? He'd have liked that...'

'Nicky's got to learn,' she said. 'I'm not a bit he's bought for his car.'

'That's obvious,' I said.

'It might be to you,' she said, and moved closer. 'Nicky's not too bright.'

'You'll be all right,' I said, feeling a rushing build in my body. I reached out and patted her shoulder. She took my hand and held it against her cheek.

'Will I?' she said.

'Yes.'

We finished our drinks.

'I like you,' she said.

'I like you too.'

'Aren't we lucky?'

'Very.'

I offered to make her some toast, but she wasn't hungry. 'Are you going to the pub?' I said.

She shook her head. 'I'd rather stay here.'

I fetched some more beer. 'It doesn't feel so creepy now?'

'Not at all.'

'It never was.'

We moved two chairs together so we could kiss. She wrapped her arms around my neck. She smelt of cow shit, but that's a pleasant, flowery smell, like hay.

She had to leave at half past ten because she was milking in the morning.

'What time?' I said.

'Seven. You going to be there?'

'Seven?'

'Yes.'

'I've got to—'

'Don't worry,' she said, laughing.

'I've got to do a load of things before I fetch Marjorie.' I showed her the list.

'Mmm,' she said.

'I'll be in trouble if I leave anything.'

'She wouldn't mind if you—'

'She would,' I said. 'And so would I.' I put the list in my pocket. 'I can be very responsible if I have to be.'

We kissed on the doorstep and she said she'd be in the pub the next evening.

'You up there every evening?' I said.

'Most, yes.'

8

Finish digging
Chop and stack wood

I did the wood first. Once I was into the rhythm of chopping I enjoyed the work. It was cold out, but I was soon warm. A stiff wind blew through the trees; the air was full of the sound of bending and whipping branches.

I could taste Sadie as I chopped, but thinking about her didn't stop me working. I barrowed four loads to the shed. Before I left for Dorchester, I stoked the Rayburn, fed the cats, tidied the kitchen and phoned Colonel Franklyn.

When he answered, he barked, 'Franklyn!' like he was shouting at himself.

I said, 'Colonel – this is Greg.'

'Greg? I don't know any Greg. Who are you?'

'Marjorie's bloke.'

'Marjorie's bloke?' He said this as if it tasted bad, but couldn't resist saying it again. 'Bloke?'

'Yes, Colonel. At the lodge. We met the other day. You were playing cards—'

'Oh!' he yelled. I held the earpiece at arm's length. 'Marjorie! Of course! I got cleaned out!' I heard him sucking his pipe. 'How is the old girl? She's—'

'I'm afraid she's in hospital,' I said. 'She's broken her arm.'

'Good God! Is she all right?'

'She's fine.'

'What happened?'

'She fell over in the kitchen. It was stupid . . . I'm just off to collect her now.'

'Good for you! Splendid. Between you and me . . . ' he lowered his voice, so I only had to hold the phone a foot away, ' . . . it's high time she had a batman.'

'I'm more of a Robin,' I said.

'I beg your pardon?'

'Robin? Batman?'

'I'm sorry,' said the Colonel. 'I don't follow.'

I excused him, and said that I was late already. 'That won't do!' he yelled, and told me to get a move on.

A nurse intercepted me on the way to Marjorie's room.

'Mr Thompson?' She put her hand on my arm.

'Yes?'

'Dr Rice would like a word with you. Could you wait in there?' She pointed to an office. 'I'll fetch him.'

'What's up?'

'I think Dr Rice should tell you.'

'OK.'

I sat in the office and tried to work out a shift rota graph. The green columns were getting the better of it in March, but the blues had the edge in April. 'Mr Thompson?' Dr Rice wore glasses and hadn't shaved. He didn't smile.

'Yes?'

'Can I ask you . . . are you a relative?'

'No.'

'What is your relationship to Miss Calder?'

'I'm just a friend of a friend. I've been working for her – chopping logs, that sort of thing.'

57

'Do you know if she has any living relatives?'
'She hasn't said anything about any.'
'I see . . . '
'Why?'
'Well . . . ' Dr Rice rubbed his chin.
'Yes?' I said.
They had run some tests on Marjorie.
'She's a remarkable woman,' he said. 'Quite a handful for the nursing staff too.'
'What's the problem?'
'Well.' Dr Rice coughed. 'It's serious. Can I ask you if you've noticed—'
'I've only known her a couple of weeks,' I said, 'but for an eighty-two-year-old she's—'
'She's got cancer.'
'Cancer?'
'I'm sorry . . . '
'Where?'
'It's pancreatic, and it's spread to the duodenum.' He took his glasses off and put them in his top pocket with a perfect, automatic action.
'No . . . '
'I'm afraid so.' He coughed softly. 'Frankly, I was appalled she hadn't been referred before, but . . . ' he tapped a sheaf of notes, ' . . . the last time she saw her GP was in 1986. Dr Thubron.'
'Who?'
'Her GP.' He looked over my shoulder for a moment, and then back at me. 'I'm afraid it's well advanced. I'm amazed she's carried on like this for so long without complaining, but as soon as I saw the blister on her eye I suspected. You'd noticed it? On her eye.'
'Yes,' I said. 'I did.'
'It's a classic symptom,' he said, like it was a car.
'Is it?'
'I'm afraid so . . . '
I hardly knew Marjorie, but this kicked me in. I

58

didn't want her to shrink, need a wheelchair, only eat baby food and die in bed. 'How long's she got?'

'Difficult to say . . . '

'Try.'

He coughed again. 'A month – three, if she's lucky.'

'Lucky?'

'I'm sorry.' Dr Rice had told this news dozens of times, but it never got any easier, only more like a cliché. That worried him.

'Does she know?'

'Not yet. We want to run a few more tests – she'll have to stay in another night. We've told her that.'

'Don't you know enough already?'

'Yes, but . . . ' He stalled. He didn't want to make a mistake.

'OK,' I said, and went to see her.

She was sitting up in bed, reading. She didn't look ill, only angry. Her face was still like a moon. When she saw me, she shook her head, put down her book and said, 'Another night. If I'm not careful they'll make me move in, and the next thing I'll know is I'm going out feet first. Except I wouldn't know that, would I?' She laughed at her joke. I couldn't. 'Did you keep the Rayburn in?'

'Yes.'

'And the cats?'

I nodded.

'And you didn't race the Alfa?'

I shook my head. I could feel tears welling up behind my eyes, and a weakness in my legs. I sat on the edge of her bed, but I couldn't look at her or say anything.

I was angry by the time I left her and was driving over the switchbacks. I was angry at the lanes to the lodge. No one deserved death by pain and shrinking, and her having cancer killed my idea that thinking about the guest inevitably led to you asking him to the party. Marjorie had slept on the ground in Australia, with deadly spiders rattling across her chest, but never been bitten. In the Congo, she had climbed a tree with some natives to escape a lioness. They'd aggravated the animal by smelling appetising. They had to stay in the tree for six hours, until a herd of antelope passed.

I was angry at the countryside, and the pretty cottages I passed. Nobody could convince me that they were worth it. I hated hedges and the twists in the road. I wanted to leave. I hated glimpses of sheep through gates, and the interesting hill forts that dominated the landscape. The sun was out, but I didn't enjoy it. When I reached the forest and accelerated into the trees, I hated the shade, and the strict way the sitkas had been planted. I wasn't interested in forest wildlife, and took no notice of warning road signs. Only the Alfa soothed me, and the feeling that I was safe in it. It was a beautiful car.

A mile from the lodge I shot round a bend and came face to face with a blue tractor. It was fifty yards from me when I first saw it – I was going too fast but I managed to stop in a straight line, six feet from it.

I wasn't reversing. I could see a pull-in behind the tractor, and edged towards it.

I honked my horn and waved. I revved. After an unnecessary wait, the tractor began to reverse.

'You took your bloody time!' I yelled as we drew level.

Nicky stuck his head out of the tractor cab and said, 'Oh, yeah?'

'Yeah!' I screamed.

Nicky laughed and pointed at the car. 'Bit of a handful for you, is it?'

'No more than I'm used to.'

He laughed again.

I would have got out and kicked him, but Marjorie's cats needed feeding, and it was getting dark. I hated the smell of his tractor. I gave him two fingers and accelerated away. He had small piggy eyes, and bad teeth. When I looked in my rear view mirror, I could see the tractor backing into the forest.

Dad died of lung cancer, and Mum of cancer of the throat; the disease was a rain in my life. I had been around both of them as they shrank: Mum took it as read and faded very quickly, but Dad refused to be beaten. Marjorie would refuse to be beaten. I spent the evening in a frenzy, making sure everything was in its place for her return. I washed the kitchen floor, vacuumed in the hall, up the stairs and along the landing. I was checking the larder for food when someone knocked on the door. It was Sadie.

'I'm sorry,' I said. 'I'm very busy.' I had a broom in my hand. 'But come in if you want.'

She did. She stood in the kitchen. I offered her a seat, but she didn't take it. She had never seen a man cleaning a house before, and I could tell that she wanted a drink, but when I explained about Marjorie, she backed off.

'Oh, I'm sorry.'

'I'm fetching her tomorrow.'

'Did you see her today?'

'Yes. She doesn't know yet.'

We stood looking at each other in silence. The Rayburn was well stoked, but the kitchen felt cold.

She said she was going. As we stood on the step, I said, 'I think I upset your boyfriend today.'

'Who's that?'

'Nicky. I made him back his tractor up. He—'

'It's about time someone made him back his tractor up,' she said.

9

Before I left the lodge to collect Marjorie from hospital I checked that everything was in its right place. Rayburn stoked – logs – cats – washing-up.

The house felt like home to me, and the time I'd spent in it on my own made me feel a belonging. It was a beautiful morning – blue skies, a few white clouds and snowdrops in the hedges.

I stopped at a garage and put the Alfa through a car-wash. When it was done, I parked it on the forecourt and checked for damage. One of the number plates was bent, but I straightened it with my boot.

Although I drove Dad to Kent and propped him in hay barns, Mum did the nursing. I qualified as a nurse when she felt an occupant in her throat, and described a burning in her mouth that made her gag and dribble.

'Look at me!' she slurred. 'I'm a baby again! Look!' I had to feed her, but she couldn't chew, so I learnt to use a liquidiser. Bruce didn't understand the change in her. I had to take him for walks, and keep him away from wheels.

He had a thing about wheels – Mum had never been strict with him – so when we passed a pushchair or shopping trolley, he went mad. Once, I let him off the lead in a park, and he chased some kids on roller skates. I had to run after all of them, but couldn't shout at him because I saw Mum reflected in his eyes. She wanted him to do the things she'd never been able to do. I always told her he behaved perfectly, and was very sensible in traffic.

She faded quickly and became very quiet, except for the last day, when she began to tell me the story of her life. She was full of memories, most of which I'd heard before, but some new ones. When she reached the end of the story, she died.

Marjorie was dressed and waiting for me in the hospital reception. She said, 'Where have you been?'

'Driving carefully.'

'Good,' she said, recognising the perfect answer – and a little of herself in me.

'Marjorie?' I said. I could see the sculptor still at it. He was cutting a stone with a high-powered electric saw. A plume of dust rose into the air.

'Let's go,' she said.

We were driving over a beautiful hump in the countryside when she turned to me and said, 'Gregory?'

'What?' I kept my eyes on the road.

'He told you, didn't he?'

'Who?'

'Dr Rice.'

'He did say some—'

'It was wonderful!' she said. 'I got one over on them! He came in to tell me – I could tell. He had this serious face, different from the "serious but you'll get better eventually" face. It was the deadly serious one. You know what I mean?'

I shook my head.

'I'm not stupid,' she said. 'I wasn't a nurse for nothing. He was winding up to break the news, but I put him out of his misery.'

'*His* misery?'
'Poor man . . .'
'Marjorie?'
'It's the other occupant.'
'The what?'
'Cancer! In my gut!'
'Oh,' I said, steering carefully. I appreciated the power assistance.
'But like I've always said . . .' she said.
'What's that, Marjorie?'
She turned away and looked at the scenery, then said, 'You take it as it comes.'

The woman loved me for keeping the lodge warm and tidy, and picked each cat up individually and kissed it.
'I'm sorry,' I said. 'I didn't go that far.'
'That's all right,' she said, and kissed me.
I wanted to cry. I pulled myself together. I had to support her. 'Support' is an old word given new meaning. I said it in my head. Marjorie sat by the Rayburn and said, 'It's wonderful to be home.' Her hair wasn't brushed, and stuck out as if she'd been plugged in. The kettle rumbled on top of the Rayburn, so I washed some cups and started to make tea.
'Nothing like a cup of tea,' I said.
'There isn't, is there?' she said, reaching for a bottle of whisky. 'Do you mix your drinks?'
'Not if I can help it,' I said.
'Then take that off,' she pointed to the kettle, 'and get some glasses.'

I was lying in bed with the lights out when I heard a noise I didn't recognise. I was used to coughing sheep, crying owls and whipping trees – this was different.

It came from the room beneath me – scratching – I listened to it for a while, trying to work out what it was. There were no trees or bushes close enough to the house to scrape against the downstairs windows – the night was solid, and the lack of other noises accentuated the scratching. When I sat up and the bed squeaked, it stopped, and all I could hear was the faint buzz of silence and an occasional hoot from the forest.

I sat up for a couple of minutes until it started again. It hadn't moved across the room, it was coming from exactly the same spot – directly beneath my bed. I don't believe in ghosts. I got out of bed, and put on a dressing gown Marjorie had lent me. It was tartan, and warm.

Marjorie hadn't lent me any slippers. The lodge was freezing. I put the landing light on. The scratching stopped. I stood at the top of the stairs and looked down. Marjorie used dim bulbs. The scratching started again.

I went down the stairs very slowly. At the bottom, I found a walking stick and armed myself with it. The noise had become more insistent. Suddenly, joining it, an owl yelled outside.

I wasn't nervous, but I was curious. I'd been in unusual and dangerous situations before – I didn't recall any of them at that moment. I opened the front room door, pushed it wide and stood on the threshold. A wall of cold air blew out of the room. The scratching stopped. I waited.

The room was dark and freezing. Nothing moved.

I advanced. I held the walking stick up and felt for the light switch. I flicked it.

The light didn't come on. I squinted into the darkness and stuck the stick out in front of me.

I moved forward. The curtains were open. Slowly my eyes got used to the light; I made out the shapes of the armchairs, an occasional table and a bookcase. My breath made light, puffy clouds; I could hear my heart beating, and feel blood rushing into my head.

'Who's there?' I said, feebly.

No answer.

'Hello?'

Through the window, the forest was a dark featureless wall. I couldn't make out the shapes of individual trees, or see any light between trunks.

I said, 'Who's there?' again and lowered the stick, and as I did, suddenly, there was a crash from the other side of the room, and a dark shape shot towards me, darted between my legs and ran into the hall.

I heard Marjorie call, 'Gregory? Is that you?'

'Yes,' I said, weakly. She was at the top of the stairs looking down.

'What's going on? I heard a noise.'

'One of the cats was in the front room.'

'Which one?'

'The black one.' I took a deep breath. 'Fred.' I put the walking stick back.

'Fred – he's a little devil.'

'He scared the life out of me,' I said, and regretted it immediately.

'You want a drink?' She came down the stairs.

'I don't know. Can't you sleep?'

'No. This . . .' she tapped her plastered arm, '. . . is ridiculous. I'll be dead before spring but I've got to heal this first.' She came down the stairs, shaking her head.

'Marjorie! Don't talk like that.'

'I won't fool myself,' she said, heading for the kitchen, 'so don't you try.'

'I—'

'Just don't.'

Dr Rice had offered Marjorie therapy on one hand and told her on the other that only one per cent of pancreatic cancer sufferers survive. She'd insisted on the facts. He said tumours had to be caught early; she was too far gone. Her cancer had eaten all it needed of her.

Dr Rice was amazed that Marjorie took it so well.

She made two cups of cocoa with one arm and pancreatic cancer.

'For the pain,' Dr Rice had said (about chemotherapy).

'Stuff your therapies,' she said, rudely. 'And blow the pain. I've had pain before.'

The doctor hadn't argued. He was a sensible thin man. He stood up, offered her his hand. She took it and he said, 'It's your decision, but if you need anything you must get in touch. I'll contact Dr Thubron personally.'

The cocoa was thick and sweet – she put a pinch of spice on top.

I had a dream that night. Marjorie and I had gone to a beach. We had a blanket. The sea was rough, but she went for a swim. There was a small boy swimming too – I watched as he dived into the waves.

I was sitting on the blanket. Seagulls were whirling above me. Marjorie shouted and waved to me. She was beyond the boy, who hadn't surfaced from his last dive. I could see his legs bobbing between the waves. They looked like aerodrome windsocks. I watched them for five minutes before thinking this wasn't right.

I stood up and pointed to him – at the same time, Marjorie noticed him.

I ran into the sea, but she reached the legs first. She grabbed the nearest foot, but when she did, her eyes widened, she noticed something on one of the toes, screamed and leapt back.

I moved forward and looked into the sea. It was

very clear, and I could see the boy's face. His arms had caught in some rocks. His lips were blue and his eyes were closed. His hair was flowing around his head like weed. He was wearing a brown swimming costume. His whole body seemed to be floating in something other than water, more like air.

10

Colonel Franklyn's Rover 95 could be spotted, like a distant posse, by the column of smoke it left in its wake. Like the man on the run, I saw him coming. I was planting beans.

Gardening is about common sense and spacing. It's common sense to cultivate the ground properly before sowing seed, but you have to look up the spacings in a book. Broad beans 'should be inserted 2 ins deep and 8 ins apart, this being the distance at which the plants will mature.'

'I used to sow them in the autumn, but I never proved the advantage,' Marjorie said.

I spent a couple of hours hoeing and raking a patch of ground before lining up and stretching a string, and then carefully sowing the seed. A few spots of rain began to blow out of the forest. It had been a dry warm winter so far. I saw the first clots of smoke from the Colonel's Rover.

When he had parked it, he climbed out and banged the bonnet. 'Wonderful bus!' he yelled. 'And all you need to keep it tip-top is a screwdriver and an adjustable spanner!' He walked towards me, and in a lowered voice said, 'That's more than you could say about hers.' He pointed to the Alfa and shook his head.

I was going to say something about his oil seals

being shot when Marjorie stuck her head out of the window and croaked, 'What about hers?'

'Marjorie!' The Colonel swung around and smiled.

'I didn't hear,' she said.

He waved over his shoulder to me, said, 'Men's talk,' and went to play cards. Half an hour later, he was forty-two Vestas down and I was washing my hands. It was raining.

Marjorie was holding a full house, he had a pair of twos, a pair of sevens and a queen. Without looking up from her cards, she said, 'You could check the loft for leaks,' to me. 'I've been waiting for the chance.'

I fetched a ladder and hauled it upstairs. The Colonel offered to help, but she told him to stay where he was.

I couldn't find any drips in the loft. It was cold up there, and the rain was loud on the slates. There were a few tea chests stacked by the hatch, but otherwise nothing.

I nagged Marjorie to phone Alice with the news, so she promised, but only if I went out. She didn't like the idea of having a conversation with an old friend and me lurking somewhere in the lodge. She didn't say this. She did say, 'Take the car if you like, but have a bath and wash your hair first.'

I drove to the pub – I felt polished. My hair was neat. I bought a pint, sat in a corner and listened to two farmers. Besides them, the barman and me, the place was empty. Someone in the neighbourhood had been fined for polluting a brook with silage effluent. The taller of the two men said, 'We made the bloody landscape they like so much, but don't mind telling us what to do with it.'

The barman was very quiet.

The other farmer said, 'You're right there.'

'It's like that copse.'
'What copse?'
'The one I scrubbed out. You know.'
The barman nodded.
'What do people want? I had them queuing to complain. And then they want cheap food.'
'You're right there.'
'The abuse! You wouldn't believe it! One of them said she was going to chain herself to one of the trees. And it's the same people who want a pile of logs for their woodburners.'
'You're right there.'
'People think they know everything.'
'They know too much,' the barman said.
'You're right there.'
'It's television. Too much bloody television. And newspapers. I've never got the time to read a paper...'
'Think of the trees in a newspaper,' said the barman.
'Yes. I wonder what those people think about that.'
'What people?'
'You know.' I was suddenly the subject of conversation. There was a little silence: the first farmer had looked at the barman; he glanced up at me and then back at his friend. He nodded. I heard a car pull into the car-park.

Nicky recognised me as soon as he came in. He was on his own. He said, 'You're the bloke in the Alfa.' His face was red and his hair lay flat on his head.

'Yeah,' I said. The farmers' conversation and the beer had given me a mellow glow that I connected to my mouth when I said, 'I'm sorry.' I could see my mistakes. 'I'd just had some bad news.'

'Bad luck,' said Nicky, meanly.

One of the farmers turned round to listen. The barman leant over the bar.

'Yes,' I said. 'It was.'

The atmosphere in the pub was thick and threatening; I felt hot though it was cold in there. 'I said I was sorry. I—'

'I heard you. What sort of bad luck?'

'You don't want to know.'

'Yes, I do,' Nicky said, and leant towards me.

The other farmer listened. Everyone listened. I said, 'I'd just heard a friend of mine has cancer. She's dying . . . '

'Marj?' said the barman.

'Yes,' I said.

Nicky leant back. 'You're staying with her?' he said.

'Yes.'

The threats vanished and I was left with four intrigued men. I had them all ears.

'She's dying?' said the barman.

'Who's dying?' said one of the farmers.

'Mad Marj.'

'Marjorie,' I said.

Nicky went to the bar for a drink. He came back, sat opposite me and drank in silence for a while, before shaking his big head and saying, 'I didn't know.'

'How could you?'

'It's a small place. Everybody knows—'

'Not as small as all that,' I said.

'That's what you think,' Nicky said.

Nicky was an overweight boy. He ate too much meat and dairy produce. I'd been listening to him talk about how he'd always felt something odd about the old gamekeeper's lodge when another car pulled up outside. He recognised it as Sadie's.

He stood up when she came in. She said, 'Hello, Nicky,' off-handedly, and then, 'Greg! You made it!' to me, excitedly.

I said, 'Yes. She kicked me out. She's phoning my Aunt Alice.'

'That's the one in Brighton?'

'Yes.'

'How's she been?'

'Excuse me—' Nicky said.

'What?' said Sadie.

'You know this bloke?'

'Greg? Yeah.'

The farmers and the barman enjoyed this twist.

'You never told me,' Nicky said to Sadie.

'Why should I?' she said, and went for a drink. 'Anyone want another?' she said.

I held my glass up. Nicky hadn't finished his.

'You didn't say anything either,' Nicky said.

I shrugged. 'What's it to you, anyway? Is she your wife or—'

'She will be.' He raised his voice. 'You can bet on that.'

'Short odds?' I said.

'I'm the favourite. No problem.'

I didn't want to argue. The day's fresh air had made me tired. When Sadie came back from the bar you could have cut the air with a knife.

I wasn't interested in proving anything, so I just sat back and listened to Nicky as he moaned about his work and told Sadie he was going to buy a sunroof for the Capri. 'You'll love it,' he said.

'Good,' she said.

Back at the lodge, Marjorie was reading a book called *Yak!* (a Tibetan adventure). She'd had a bath, and was in her dressing gown, sitting by the Rayburn.

'Nice drink?' she said.

'The beer was good. How's Alice?'

'Fine.' She went back to her book. 'She sends her love.'

'Did you tell her?'

'What's there to tell?'

'I thought that's why you were phoning her. You said—'

Marjorie held her good hand up and said, 'Don't worry. She knows.' She pointed to the whisky. 'Have a drink.'

Mum drank as she died. She'd always avoided spirits, but rum became one of the few things she could swallow.

Once she gave some to Bruce, 'because he watches me when I pour a glass. It's like he's asking for a tot.' Then she asked me to take the dog for a stroll.

I took the dog for a drag. When we reached the garden gate and I put the lead on, he lay down, so I had to carry him to the park. I put him on the grass and dragged him around until a woman came over and threatened me with violence unless I stopped being cruel. I didn't say anything about Mum having cancer, but I did say that she'd got the dog drunk, and that if she hassled Mum about it, I wouldn't be responsible for Mum's actions. Then I picked Bruce up and carried him home.

11

When Marjorie began to sleep late I offered to take her breakfast in bed. At first, she told me not to be stupid. She had never had breakfast in bed before, and wasn't starting because she was dying. I told her that because she was dying she should indulge herself. She appreciated my frankness, and because of it said yes, she would have breakfast in bed.

She liked cereal, toast, marmalade and a pot of tea. I would have mine first, before carrying hers up and sitting beside her while she ate.

'I'm decadent,' she said.

'You're ill.'

'That's no excuse.' She let me pour milk into her cereal. 'I don't like excuses. If you've got to use an excuse it means you've made a mistake.'

'No, it doesn't!'

'Are you arguing with me, Gregory?'

'Yes.'

'Well, excuse me,' she said. I couldn't do anything with her.

It became important to her to visit places in the area she would never see again. She made me fetch a pile of guide books and two maps and chose. One day it was Sleech Wood, Rhode Barton and Hole Common, another it was Bettiscombe (home of the Screaming Skull of Bettiscombe Manor) and Coney's Castle.

In 833, King Egbert the Great of Wessex lived at

Coney's Castle. We stood on a grassy plateau, and as litter blew all around, we imagined him receiving emissaries from East Anglia, Mercia and Northumbria. For the first time in England's history, the excuse of invasion had spurred the disparate kingdoms to unite: the Danes had already ravaged the north and east. Wessex provided the last bastion, and the first king of all England. Egbert watched for invasion. He had a righteous wife (name unrecorded), mother of Ethelwulf and grandmother of Ethelbald, Ethelbert, Ethelred and Alfred. Marjorie and I watched a pair of horses in a field below, and saw kestrels hovering over the escarpments. In the distance, a bypass was being built around Charmouth. The fresh cuttings were pale, and shone in the sunshine. Marjorie taught me to appreciate nature.

'We'll do the Undercliff tomorrow,' she said.

'You'll wear yourself out,' I said.

She laughed. 'Were you born stupid?' she said.

'No.'

'So you're self-taught?'

'No!'

'What then?'

We did the Undercliff – a wood between Lyme and Axmouth that falls off the fields to the north and tumbles into the sea. A muddy path meanders through it for five miles. We managed two and a half, but in such an inaccessible place, we met weird people.

We must have looked weird. I was wearing battle fatigues; she took me with one arm, the other, plastered and slung, swung and bounced against her chest. We didn't hurry. We met a motorcyclist on the tarmacked lane that led down to the woods. He stopped to let us pass, and yelled, 'It's a stoater!'

'What?' I shouted.

Marjorie didn't say anything. She was staring at the sky. It was deep blue; a few clouds moved across it like brides and grooms to the altar, or tears down a cheek. The man turned his bike off and leant back in the saddle like Marlon Brando. I whistled through my teeth. He spoke to Marjorie.

'A stoater! Brilliant! Today! It's brilliant!'

Marjorie said, 'It certainly is.'

'Yes,' I said.

The man needed a shave. He had a knapsack slung over his shoulder and his boots had holes in them. He kicked the bike on again and said, 'I'm late.'

'Oh, we can't have that,' said Marjorie, laughing.

The man laughed too, and then rode away.

The wood was nothing like the forest around the lodge. It was more of a jungle – enormous sycamore, ash and beech trees grew out of tangles of brambles and gorse. Creepers climbed into the branches of the trees, birds called alarms, and all around us the undergrowth rustled as mice and voles dived for cover. The path was well trodden. Every now and again we glimpsed the sea between the branches; we could hear it all the way.

We were climbing a flight of steps cut into a bank that crossed the path when I heard a loud human yelling. It was insistent – not in pain, but needing something. After a minute, it was joined by another scream, then another and another until somewhere in the woods below us a group of people were filling the air with their cries.

'What the hell is that?' I said.

'I don't know,' Marjorie said. 'But it reminds me of something. I . . . ' She stopped and thought.

'It's down there.' I pointed.

'OK,' she said. 'Let's find out what,' and she began to crash through the undergrowth towards it.

We beat our way through brambles, clematis and clumps of hazel until we reached a small path, less muddy than the main one. Marjorie orientated herself on it, brushed her trousers and waited for me to catch up. The yelling stopped for a moment. She whispered, 'In the Congo. That's where it was. God! I must be losing my memory. Memory . . . I thought that was the last thing to go!'

'Marjorie?' I said.

'Come on!' The noise started again. 'This way.'

The way her broken arm was set threw the rest of her body into an uncomfortable arch, her back hunched. I followed this down the small path. All around us, trees and bushes were bursting their buds. Somewhere in front of us, people were bursting their veins. As we got closer, I could make out individual cries. Some were men and some were women.

'The Congo,' Marjorie said. 'The M'Bochi used to put on shows for us. They screamed like that.' She had stopped for a breather. I caught up with her. 'Evil spirits,' she said.

I stood beside her and puffed.

'Gregory,' she said.

'What?'

'I'm the one who's dying.'

'Very funny,' I said.

'I thought so.'

We walked for another hundred yards before Marjorie suddenly stopped, crouched and signalled for me to join her.

I crouched next to her and parted some branches so I could see. There were a dozen people standing around a huge beech tree with their heads thrown back, yelling at the tops of their voices. There was no wildlife in the area. The grass around the tree was well trodden. Most of the men had beards, and the women had long hair. Marjorie was fascinated, and wanted to ask them what was going on.

'It's religious,' I said.

'Of course it's religious,' she said, and waited for them to stop.

'They might not want to be disturbed.'

They stopped. Marjorie stood up and walked towards them. I stayed where I was. She made a lot of noise climbing out of our hiding place and crashing into the clearing, but none of the screamers moved. They stared into the branches of the beech tree.

'Hello,' Marjorie said.

No one said anything.

'We were walking – we heard you and thought there might be someone in trouble, but . . . '

One of the men looked away from the branches and at us. None of the others moved. They were transfixed – I didn't know what to do with myself but Marjorie was confident. The man said, 'That's beautiful.'

'We didn't mean to disturb you . . . ' said Marjorie.

'No,' said the man. 'It was beautiful of you to come. Thank you.'

'No thanks,' Marjorie said.

'Really.' The man put his hands together and bowed to us, said, 'Thank you,' again and then went back to his place, closed his eyes, opened his mouth and let out another scream. The others waited for a moment before joining him.

We walked away from the clearing and back to the main path. While Marjorie talked about the Congo, I remembered some hippies in London who had promised themselves that scene.

'Primal screaming,' Marjorie said. 'They're letting it all out so they can get back to their beginnings. It was the same with the M'Bochi. The M'Bochi had style though.'

'What's style got to do with it?'

'Everything. Do it in style, I say,' she said.

'I say it's bollocks,' I said.

'You would.'

'Would I?'

'Yes.'

We walked as far as a pumping station where the path ran through a grove of trees and led down to the beach. Huge rocks were scattered on the beach. There were patches of fine shingle. We sat down to eat a picnic.

'I used to come here when I first lived at the lodge. The best beach for miles,' Marjorie said. 'No one comes here.'

'We're here.'

'If they do,' she said, ignoring my remark, 'it's because they mean to. They've looked for it. Like minds,' she mumbled, and watched a fishing boat.

I watched her. The edge of her plaster, where it met her hand, was disintegrating and grey. She refused to take the doctor's advice and take it easy, but had the best reason not to. She knew the boat was crabbing. The sun was high and bright, but not hot. Behind us, a pipe that ran from the pumping station was throwing fresh water on to the beach. I said, 'You know all the best places, Marjorie.'

'How do you know?'

'I was just saying it as a—'

'Say away,' she said. 'Just don't imagine you think you know what I know.'

I looked at her. She closed her eyes. I looked at the sea. The waves reminded me of my dream, but I didn't want to bore her. They puddled in pools beyond the shingle. A few birds were pecking around their edges; when I looked back at Marjorie, for a moment I thought she was dead, but when I looked closer I could see her breathing and a small smile crept on to her face.

The walk back to the car became a struggle for Marjorie. By the time we reached it, it was getting dark, and she was exhausted.

'What a day,' she mumbled, as I helped her into

the seat and did up her belt. 'I want to keep every day. Every minute. Now I know I'm dead . . . '

'You're not—'

'Don't say it! Just don't say anything!'

I drove home slowly and didn't bicker. She was asleep by the time we reached the lodge. I woke her gently, and when she was ready, she climbed out of the car. She refused my arm, but didn't mind when I offered to make her a bottle and some cocoa. She was in bed when I took them to her, and for the first time I noticed a thinning in her face and a weakness in her voice. The blister on her eye was bigger than I had seen it before. She covered it with her good hand, and sighed.

'Gregory?' she said.

'Yes?'

'I don't think we'll go anywhere tomorrow.' She sipped some cocoa. 'There're too many places I have to see anyway. I can't see them all. You chop some wood.'

'Marjorie?'

'You can never chop enough wood.'

She put the cup to her lips again, but lost her grip and spilt it down her front and over the bed. 'Agh!' she cried.

I grabbed a towel from a chair and began to wipe the mess, but she grabbed it and shouted, 'It's all right! I can manage!'

'I—'

'Let me do it!' I backed off. 'Go on!'

'I'll fetch—'

'Fetch nothing! Just get out!'

'Marjorie . . . '

'*Get!*' she screamed.

I stood outside the door and listened to her get out of bed. She went to her chest of drawers – I heard one open. I heard her curse her bad arm. Five minutes later I heard the bedsprings squeak as she got back in. I went downstairs and drank my cocoa.

A strong wind had begun to blow through the forest. Where it met the right conditions, it threw up little whirls of pine needles and cones, and flung them into clearings. The sky was clear and the moon shone brightly, so the trees looked like bars and bars, stretching away to nothing.

12

I was in the newsagent in Charmouth, looking for lettuce seed. They had a dozen different varieties. They called themselves a newsagent, but you could also buy cigarettes, nails, fire cheeks, binoculars, dolls, fishing tackle, *Tess of the d'Urbervilles*, dog collars, electric drills, alarm clocks, garden forks, maps, etc., there. I chose a packet of Cos lettuce seed and took it to the counter. As I was paying, Sadie came into the shop.

I had never seen her in a skirt before; she was also wearing red socks. I said, 'Hello, Sadie.'

She smiled and said, 'Hello. How are you?'

'OK,' I said.

She had seen me in the shop as she drove past – she didn't want to buy anything. She said, 'Have you been to the beach?'

'Which one?'

'Here.'

'No.'

'You want to see it?'

'OK.'

'Let's go, then.'

I didn't argue.

It wasn't far. We walked down a quiet road, past a school, the village hall and a playing field, to where an empty car-park was being used as a building site. An excavator was working in a field beside the river that ran into the sea, digging a trench for a new sewage pipe. We crossed a bridge over a lagoon, said, 'Excuse me,' to some people who were tossing bread at some ducks and walked past signs warning about pollution on the beach.

The sea was coming in in high, steaming rollers; there was no fishing boat out today. The beach was long and wide. Sadie picked up some stones, threw them into the waves and ran back when the water rushed up to catch her feet. When I caught up with her, she took my arm and snuggled against me as we walked. It was windy.

'Sorry about Nicky last week,' she said.

'What did he do?'

'In the pub . . . you remember.'

'That? You don't have to apologise.'

'I know. But—'

'Sadie,' I said. 'You're falling into his trap. You think you're responsible for him.'

'I—'

'If you don't like him, forget him. Go somewhere else. You don't have to go to the same pub every night. You—'

'I know. I—'

'Sadie.' I stopped walking and turned her to face me. She didn't want to look at me. 'Make your own choices,' I said. 'You don't owe anybody anything.'

She hung her head for a moment before lifting it, sweeping her hair from her face and saying, 'I know.'

'Then do it,' I said.

'But what's it?'

'Make your own mind up about that one. I can't help you there.' I shook my head. 'Choose.'

'Choose?'

'That's it.'

We walked beneath tall, crumbling cliffs. Rivers of

blue mud ran off the fields above us, down the cliffs, across the beach and into the sea. A few men were chipping at rocks that were lying around.

'I'd choose you,' she said.

'What?'

'I'd choose you, given the choice.'

'Between what?'

'Any of the blokes around here.'

'Sure,' I said.

'What?'

I stopped this time. 'Nothing. I'm sorry. I'm just tired.'

'Marjorie been working you hard?'

'I suppose so.'

'How is she?'

'Not too good. She loses patience with herself. It wouldn't be so bad if she had two arms.'

'I think it would be just as bad.'

Clouds raced above us; in a gap between them I saw an aeroplane trail across blue sky. 'I suppose so,' I said.

We came to a place where flat rocks lay on the shore, and we sat down. Sadie threaded her arms around me and kissed my cheek. I could tell she wanted more, but I didn't feel like it. I was enjoying the sound of the waves, and the sight of the gulls tumbling through the grey sky. The scene was wild and desolate, and from that shore you could get the feeling of power in nature. She was used to it.

'I'm sorry,' I said. 'I'm not myself today. Give me a day or two and I'll . . . '

'What's the matter?'

' . . . I'll take you out. Fancy it?'

She brightened at this. 'Wednesday?' she said.

'OK. Where do you want to go?'

'I don't know. Surprise me.'

As we walked back, a cold, driving drizzle blew

off the sea, and though it was very fine we soon got soaked.

I sowed the lettuce in seed trays in Marjorie's greenhouse. It was pleasant working in there as it rained. The smells were earth, creosote and rust. I did as I was told: sift the compost, spread in clean trays, sow the seed thinly.

The rain ran down the glass in torrents, but none leaked in. When I'd finished, I washed my hands and had a cup of tea.

'You must think I'm mad,' Marjorie said. She was drinking whisky at half past two in the afternoon. I had moved a sofa into the kitchen. She was lying on it with the cats on top of her.

'Why?'

'Planting a vegetable garden when I'm not going to live to see it grow.'

'It's me that's doing the planting,' I said.

'You know what I mean.'

She insisted on buying decent tea. That afternoon, I was drinking a China Caravan blend. 'I had wondered,' I said, 'but I don't think you're mad.'

'It's what you've got to do,' she said.

'Exactly.'

'Life goes on.'

'Doesn't it?'

In the last months of his life, apart from developing a taste for car trips to Kent, Dad took up smoking. When she first met him, Mum had been attracted to his fresh smell and his healthy lungs. As he died, he decided to see 'what's in it', and bought a packet of Woodbines. He smoked one, puked up and threw the rest away.

'Odd thing to do,' he said to me later, and Mum reminded him that she liked his fresh smell. He laughed at that, said to her, 'I smell rotten,' and said to me, 'When I'm gone, make sure she gets herself a dog.'

13

I met Sadie in a pub in Charmouth, but she didn't want to stay there, so we drove to a wine bar in Bridport.

She loved the car and said, 'You're a better driver than Nicky. He's a show-off.'

'Is he?'

'Yes.' She leant forward and fiddled with the radio. 'But you don't want to hear about him, do you?'

'No,' I said. 'If it's not you, it's Marjorie.'

There was a spontaneous atmosphere in the wine bar that spilled over us. Some people called The Brid Valley Formation Drinking Team were drinking pints, chasing these with shorts, and playing with ravioli. One of them sang an obscene song about a parrot while the others balanced glasses on their heads.

After I'd drunk a few glasses of wine, eaten some lasagna, and complained about the noise, the team suggested that I sing a song.

'I can't sing,' I said.

'You've got a voice, haven't you?' one slurred.

'Yes.'

'Ask him if he knows any songs.'

'Do you know any songs?'

'Of course I do.'

'Then sing.'

The Formation Team were waiting. Other customers

looked at me. I was sensible. I sang 'Your Letters', an old number none of them had heard of:

> Empty eyes, empty books,
> Empty beds, empty looks,
> Faceless photographs that I took,
> Of you standing with your empty look.
>> This is all that memory can offer,
>> The memory part of love gets tougher
>> and rougher every day;
>> I remember your letters.
> The rhyming part of our lives has gone,
> Everything we do someone else has done,
> I don't remember you ever telling me,
> That I was your ship on a sinking sea.
>> This is all that memory can offer,
>> The memory part of love gets tougher
>> and rougher every day;
>> I remember your letters.

I sang loudly, hit all the high notes, and phrased the verses with feeling. The applause was rapturous. The owner fetched me a bottle of wine but didn't offer me a job. Sadie said, 'That was great.'

'Was it?'

'Yes,' and she stuck her tongue in my mouth.

One of the Formation Team came over, spilt his beer over a friend, waited for Sadie to finish, slapped me on the back and said, 'Nice one!'

The slap winded me, but I managed to wheeze, 'No problem.'

I was sharing the wine with Sadie and the people on the next table when a couple approached. 'Sadie? That you?' said the woman.

'Jo!' said Sadie. 'Reg!'

Jo and Reg were young farmers who enjoyed a laugh. They thought I was one. In a huddle, I heard Jo say,

'He's nice,' to Sadie, meaning me. Reg said something about a fertiliser spinner, but I didn't know what he was talking about. He was a huge man, but quiet. He asked me where I came from, what I did and how long I was staying. I couldn't answer any of these questions, but he didn't seem to mind.

He told me about ratios of nitrate relative to the season, and thought I was interested. He wanted me to have another drink, but I said, 'No, thanks, I'm driving.'

Jo heard this and said, 'He's a good boy,' to Sadie. She agreed. She had another glass of wine and slipped her arm around my waist. I put one of my hands between her legs.

I drove and Sadie directed. We left the main road outside Bridport, and drove through Symondsbury, Broadoak and up to Shave Cross. Just before Whitchurch Canonicorum, she told me to slow down and watch for a gateway. She wanted to check some sheep . . . 'There!' she said, and slapped my knee. I parked.

'Come on,' she said. 'You can help me.'

'With what?'

'Counting!' She laughed. 'I was never any good at maths.'

'Nor was I. I was hopeless.'

'Great!' she said. 'We've got something in common.'

'We've got lots in common,' I said, but she was gone.

It was dark. I followed her over the gate and across a muddy field. She had drunk too much – I was just under my limit. The moon was waning but bright. The grass was sodden. A few sheep weren't interested in us. Sadie wasn't interested in them. We came to a stone shed by a gate. She kicked the door open and said, 'Hey! Look at this!'

'What?' I joined her.

'Looks comfy, doesn't it?' she said, and pointed to some broken bales of straw that lay scattered around the floor. She took my hand and led me in.

As soon as she'd shut the door, she threw her arms around me and kissed my neck and lips. I stroked the back of her head. A small window threw a chapter of moonlight on to the floor.

'Here,' she moaned, and stuck one of my hands up her shirt. 'Like that?'

'Yes,' I said.

'Is that all?'

'No. It's great.' I squeezed her.

She put one of her knees between my legs and shoved against me for a moment before breaking away and saying, 'Wait a minute.'

'Why?' I whispered.

'Here.' She went to a pile of unbroken bales in the corner of the barn, and pulled out a blanket. 'Straw gets in all the wrong places,' she said.

'I bet.'

She laid the blanket over the straw and took her trousers off. She was naked by the time I got mine off, and waiting for me. In the moonlight I could see her hair, part of her neck, one breast, some of her stomach, one thigh, both her knees and a foot. I lay down.

She was enthusiastic and athletic, and grunted like a pig. You never know what you're going to find out about a woman when you get naked. When she was dressed she seemed sad and insecure. When I was dressed, she thought I was cool. When we were naked she was wild and I was cold. I rubbed my arms and legs.

'That's my job,' she said. 'And you do me. Remember?'

Some straw worked its way on to the blanket, and

when she got me on my back, it irritated me. She took my squirming for lust, and pinned me down, like I was a groundsheet.

'Go on, then,' I said. 'Ride me!'

'Where to?'

'Fool!' I said.

'That feel foolish?' she said, and clenched me.

'No . . .'

'What about that?'

I shook my head, but couldn't say anything, as a gap opened in my heart.

We ground into each other for half an hour before the climax. I had never met a naked woman like her. It was the fresh air, or dairy produce, or animals mating in the fields. She screamed, dug her finger nails into my back and bit my neck. At the time this didn't hurt. I bruised her buttocks.

As we were walking back to the car, I trod in some sheep shit. We resolved to meet again, but I said, 'Let's find somewhere comfortable next time.'

'Wasn't that?'

'Yes. But . . .' I fiddled with my trousers. 'That bloody straw gets everywhere.'

'I know! But you've just got to learn to avoid it. It's easy when you know how.'

'I'll take your word for it.'

'That and an aspirin,' she said.

'What? Have you got a headache?'

'No, Greg. Not a headache.'

Three

14

Hardown Hill, a few miles from the old lodge, is one of the hills that dominate the landscape of West Dorset. Although it's skirted by the A35, it's a wild, reminding place, shaped like a blackbird's head, or a potato.

Marjorie remembered it as 'Gorse, heather and broom. Windy too. Very windy.' She wiped her eyes with a handkerchief. 'Take me there, Gregory,' she said.

She had been suffering pains in her gut, and headaches, but she insisted. She refused to let me help her do anything – get dressed, get down the stairs, eat breakfast . . .

I was eating muesli when she came into the kitchen carrying a shotgun. 'Gregory,' she said. 'If it ever gets to the point where I need help dressing, I want you to use this on me.' She propped it against the larder door and sat down.

'Come on!' I said.

She smiled. 'No,' she said. 'Don't worry.'

'I didn't know you had a gun.'

'There's a lot of things you don't know about me.'

'What do you use it for?'

'Protection,' she said. 'The garden needs protection. Wait till those beans come up and you'll see what I mean.'

'The garden?'

She helped herself to cereal. 'Yes. Nature's wild. Tooth and claw, you know?'

'I noticed.'

She sat down and ate slowly. She pointed to my neck with her spoon. 'How's Sadie?'

'OK.'

'Are you going steady?'

'Not really.'

'What does that mean?'

I shrugged, made some toast and asked her, 'Did you ever live with anyone?'

'A long time ago,' she said, after a pause. 'Before the war.' Another pause. 'We thought everything was going to be different for us.'

'What was he like?'

Marjorie laughed then, louder than I'd heard her laugh before, but with a scary rattle that vibrated through the laugh and swamped it. Then she had a coughing fit and spat into a handkerchief I fetched.

I said, 'What's the joke?'

She drank some tea, put her hand on her stomach, winced and said, 'Nothing's funny, Gregory. That's the trouble. It's not even funny any more.'

'What's not funny any more?'

'I'll tell you later,' she said, but never did.

I parked in a convenient parking space with a view of the fields and woods around Bridport, and we began the slow, hard climb to the top of Hardown Hill. It was deserted, and the nature different from any I'd seen before. 'Ancient places,' Marjorie said. 'Real old heathland, this place. The blasted heath . . .'

'It's windy,' I said.

'Blasted.'

The view from the top telescoped and circled out

to sea and inland. There was an old burial mound we stood next to.

Hardown Hill is owned by the National Trust. It was 'Open to the public (subject to the by-laws on the back of this notice). Please avoid leaving litter, lighting fires, damaging trees or plants.'

By-law 13: 'No unauthorised person shall pitch, erect or permit to remain on Trust property any tent, booth, windbreak, pole, clothes line, building, shed, post, fence, railing or other erection or obstruction whatsoever.'

Just below the summit of the hill, a huge aerial and a fake stone-clad building had been erected. 'Look at it,' Marjorie said. The aerial was for people with car phones. A sign on the door stated, 'This building is occupied by Racal Vodafone Ltd, The Courtyard, Newbury, Berks, RG13 1JL.' Another sign shouted, DANGER HIGH VOLTAGE. Three clad coaxial cables led from the building to the aerial. The installation was surrounded by high chain-link fencing, topped with barbed wire.

'Do you trust the National Trust?' Marjorie said.

'Who are they?' I said.

'You must know!'

I shook my head.

She thought that was funny.

We found a seat and sat down. The wind was stronger than ever, and blew Marjorie's hat off. I fetched it, and handed it back to her. Her hair was streaming out.

All the fat had left her face, so her nose looked like a chip of ice. Her cheeks were hollow and her mouth was pinched. Little spots of dried blood sat along the top of her bottom lip. Her eyes were wide open against the wind. She had a blister on each of them now, and they were absolutely dry. I put my arm around her shoulder and said, 'Warm enough, Marjorie?'

She nodded, but didn't look at me.

We sat for an hour. My heart played a slow tune, more like words than music. She was saying goodbye, so I didn't say anything. It was a painful, bitter wind, but after a while I didn't notice it. I felt like I was being washed. The car phone aerial whistled all the time.

A kestrel struggled to keep steady, hovering over a field below us, but level with us.

'It's a bloody shame,' she said.

'What?'

'I think about the future. I'm happily making plans – I forget . . . ' Her voice trailed away.

'There'll always be—'

'I've always made plans,' she said, ignoring me. 'I used to love thinking about what I was going to do next. Where I was going. I used to lie in bed before I went to sleep, deciding, deciding . . . ' She sucked her lips in. 'It's funny. I was coming here with you. No one could have predicted that, could they?'

I shook my head. It was cold, and I was cold deep down, like ice caves had opened in my belly and yawned at my organs and bones, and my blood.

'Maybe I'm still going somewhere . . . ' she said.

'To a better place?' I said.

She shook her head. 'There couldn't be a better place than the earth.'

I snorted.

She smiled. 'There's nothing like dying to concentrate the goodness in things.'

'Isn't there?'

'No. I think it's underrated.'

'What?'

'Dying. I'm quite enjoying it.'

The kestrel gave up. It was caught by a gust that met us a moment later, and blew it up in a huge arc. It tumbled out of this and disappeared behind a hedge.

We walked back slowly. She leant on me all the way, and we had to stop a few times, but when we crossed a muddy patch in the path that sloped too far, she slipped, I slipped, and we lay in the mud together. I laughed, but when I sat up and looked at her, she was crying. 'Look at me!' she said. She propped herself on her elbows, but couldn't get up any further. 'And I'm stuck.'

I stood up, put my arms under her shoulders and lifted, but when she tried to stand, she slipped into the mud again.

National Trust By-law 22: OBSCENE LANGUAGE. 'No person shall on Trust property use any indecent or obscene language to the annoyance of any person.'

I had to carry Marjorie. She was freezing, wet,, muddy and crying. 'No fucking dignity!' she cried. 'That's the only thing I can't stand!'

'Marjorie,' I said. 'You've got more fucking dignity that anyone I've met before.'

When we reached the car, I helped her into her seat, and when she turned to thank me, I saw Dad's face in hers. This startled me, and when I was sitting in the car and the wind wasn't blowing, I felt light, and then suddenly very heavy. I couldn't move for five minutes, but Marjorie didn't ask why. She just sat and stared at the scenery.

'Once more,' she said eventually. 'Drive back through Birdsmoorgate.'

I stopped beside the cottage we'd parked by before. She didn't want to get out of the car, but she wanted to be on her own for a while, so I pointed up the road and said, 'I'll walk to the top.' It was starting to drizzle, but I didn't mind.

*

When we got back to the lodge, I sat her by the Rayburn and she said, 'I don't think I can walk any more.'

'Of course you can—'

'I said,' she rattled, 'that I can't walk any more.'

We had some tea before I ran her a bath, carried her upstairs and sat her in the bathroom. 'Shout if you need me,' I said.

'I won't,' she said, and didn't.

When I took her breakfast in the morning, she looked as sick as I'd seen her. I left the tray on her bed, opened the curtains and said, 'Take your time.' She scratched her face, straightened her hair and nodded, but didn't say anything.

I went back half an hour later. The tray hadn't been touched. I offered to pour her some tea, but she shook her head and said, 'I feel very tired today.'

'I'm going to call the doctor,' I said.

'No, you're not,' she whispered.

'I will—'

'I won't let you.'

'You can't stop me.'

'I can!' She tried to sit up, but couldn't.

I went downstairs.

'Gregory!'

I phoned Dr Thubron. He was surprised I hadn't phoned earlier, and came as soon as he could. By that time Marjorie had seen sense, but wasn't happy when he insisted on admitting her to hospital. 'Even if it's just for a fresh plaster,' he said. He shivered at the cold. 'It's freezing in here.'

'We live in the kitchen,' I said. 'Maybe I should make a bed for her in there.'

'Gregory,' he said. 'I doubt very much that she'll be coming home this time.'

'She's—'
'Has she got any relatives?'
'I don't think so.'
'Mmm,' he said.
'Is it important?'
'Not really. If it's not to her . . .'
'I don't think it is.'
'I'm not surprised.'

15

Mum didn't enjoy dying, but she never had Marjorie's ideas. Marjorie never had children. She never worried about what other people thought. Mum was more worried about what neighbours would think if they saw her dribbling than she was about her own comfort. I told her to 'Screw the neighbours. They know sod all.'

'Mrs Harris is captain of a Scrabble team!' she protested.

'Mrs Harris only gives you the time of day because you're dying. She wants people to think she cares.'

'She—'

'Everybody knows she doesn't.'

The doctor offered Mum a Zimmer frame, but she pointed to me and said, 'Can a Zimmer cook breakfast?'

The doctor shook his head.

'He can,' Mum said, and slapped me on the back.

One evening, we watched television until closedown. Mum prodded Bruce when adverts for dog food came on, but he didn't watch them. He was satisfied with fresh meat.

She said, 'I wish I'd got away more, in my life . . .'

'What do you mean? Where?'

'I always fancied America.'

'You never said.'

'What was the point? We couldn't have gone, anyway. It was just a dream.'

'Those sort of dreams are only sent to worry you. You wouldn't have enjoyed it if you'd gone.'

'How do you know?'

'I know you, Mum. You're only happy at home.'

'Do you take after me, Greg?'

'Maybe,' I said. 'I like a home.'

I drove Marjorie to Dorchester Hospital, and sat with her on the ward. A nurse plumped up some pillows and said, 'What have we been doing with ourselves, then?'

'Trying to get on with our life,' Marjorie croaked.

'Oh dear,' said the nurse.

'It just won't do, will it?' Marjorie said.

She had caught a cold. Her gut was burning a hole in her body, and she had a headache all the time. Her arm was broken in two places and she couldn't walk. She laughed at the nurse, but the woman wasn't offended.

I wanted to stay, but Marjorie said, 'There's work to do.' I didn't want a sermon, so I went home, but I left a piece of my heart with her.

When I visited in the morning, she pleaded with me to get her out. They had put her on strong drugs, and she didn't want to end up like a cabbage.

'They're just for the pain,' I said. 'My dad had stuff just like it.'

'I don't care what your dad had!'

'He—'

'Just get me out of here!'

'If you asked, they'd discharge you without—'

'I already did.'

'And?'

She shook her head. 'They want me to die here. They like to keep all the messes in one place.'

'Marjorie!'

'Get me out of here,' she hissed.

'All right. But how—'

'I don't know. Think!'

'OK, Marjorie.'

I saw this in a film: two people and a dummy in a wheelchair visit a patient. Behind curtains drawn around the patient's bed, the two people swap the dummy for the patient and steal him away. On the way out of Dorchester Hospital, I saw a row of unattended wheelchairs.

On the way to the lodge, I called on Sadie. Her mother answered the door. I explained who I was. Her mother said, 'Oh, yes.' She looked up and down, leant towards me and said, 'Sadie hasn't stopped talking about you.'

'Oh,' I said.

'No! Don't sound so glum!' She grinned. 'I haven't seen her so happy for ages!'

Sadie's mother was in control. She pointed towards a yard behind the house. 'She's milking. I'm sorry I can't show you the way, but I've got my hands full.' She held them up. 'Marmalade.'

'OK,' I said. 'Thanks.'

The milking parlour smelt of clean water. The cows weren't interested in me. They moved slowly and were bigger close up than they where when you saw them in a field. There was nothing dangerous and bad-tempered about them, but I kept my distance. Every one was different.

The noise of the machines was echoed by rhythmic jets of milk that shot along pipes which ran up and then down into large glass jars lining the walls. I watched for a minute before Sadie saw me.

She worked quickly and confidently, occasionally patting the side of an animal's leg, or gently prodding an udder. I said, 'I've never been in one of these places before.'

'We had some school kids once', she said, flushing a pound of feed into a hopper, 'who thought you had to kill them to get the milk out. They wanted to know where the knives were.'

'I don't believe you.'

'It's true! Honestly.' She yanked an overhead lever and let three cows out. 'You'd be surprised. Some people can't put two and two together.'

'That's true.'

'You bet it is.'

I'd never seen a cow being milked before. I wasn't embarrassed, but like a film you're told is great and you think it is until you see it, I was intrigued until I got bored. The parlour was noisy and wet. Cows didn't look before pissing or shitting – Sadie was expert at keeping an eye out.

When the last cow was done, I helped her sweep the holding yard before asking if she would help me.

'Why?'

I explained the plan.

'Excitement!' she said.

'Yes. But we've got to think it through. No mistakes.'

'No mistakes,' she said.

We made a dummy out of pyjamas stuffed with straw, a white stocking filled with straw for the head, bandages, a hat and a blanket. I went back to the lodge and stoked the Rayburn, fed the cats, tidied Marjorie's bedroom, put bottles in her bed and washed the dishes. I picked Sadie up after she'd had some tea.

Her father came out to meet me. He was a small man with a bone-crushing handshake. He wore a frayed hat, hadn't shaved and drove a BMW. He said, 'Weren't you skittling with Nicky tonight?' to Sadie.

'Tell him I've got something important on.'

'Please?'

'Please.'

'You didn't say anything about Nicky,' I said.

'He doesn't own me. You said that.'

The dummy was in the boot. I drove carefully, while Sadie said things had been so exciting and romantic since I'd arrived in the Vale. The less I said, and the more I tried to disagree, the more exciting (and romantic) it was for her. I couldn't win. She put her hand on my thigh but I slapped it away. 'Later,' I said. 'We've got to get Marjorie home first. Concentrate on one thing at a time. That's the first rule of coping with excitement. OK?'

'OK,' she said, and smiled.

'Good.'

At the hospital, I fetched one of the unattended wheelchairs. No one was watching them. I just strolled past a photograph of Prince Charles and helped myself. We took a lot of time arranging the dummy to look right. We tucked the blanket around its feet, and bowed its head. The hat covered the features it didn't have. I pushed. Sadie took my arm.

We took a crowded lift to the first floor. The people with us sniffed the air – a doctor said, 'I can smell sheep,' and looked at a colleague. 'Can you smell sheep?'

'Yes,' said the colleague, and looked down at the dummy. I shook my head. The doors opened, we wheeled out, turned left, passed a wall of modern paintings and I held the doors while Sadie pushed the chair on to Marjorie's ward. 'Wait in there,' I said. There was a visitors' waiting room. 'I'll check with the nurses.'

Two of the nurses were undernourished, three wore glasses and the sixth was busy. I explained about Marjorie's friend being in a wheelchair, but the two women had been friends for over sixty years, and she'd insisted on coming in. 'Five minutes,' said the chief nurse. 'It's past visiting hours . . . ' She looked at her watch.

'That's very kind of you,' I said.

One of the nurses offered to close the curtains around Marjorie's bed. I said, 'No. We can manage,' and fetched Sadie.

No one looked twice as we wheeled the dummy into Marjorie's room, and closed the curtains. It had been a busy day in Dorchester Hospital. I woke Marjorie gently.

'Who?' she croaked.

'Ssh,' I said, and pointed at the dummy. 'We've come for you.'

I pointed at Sadie. Sadie smiled. 'Hello,' she said.

'Who?' said Marjorie.

'Sadie,' I said. 'And Gregory. Come on.'

She was very weak, but strong enough to understand what she had to do. I got her out of bed and sat her on the edge while Sadie took the dummy out of the wheelchair and arranged it realistically under the sheets and blanket.

Marjorie didn't want to wear the dummy's hat, but I explained that it was essential. 'You want to go home, don't you?' I said.

'Yes.'

'Then wear it.'

'It's filthy!'

'Wear it!' I hissed.

She put it on, but scowled at me.

As we were leaving the ward, I said to the chief nurse, 'She's asleep.'

'Who?'

'Marjorie.'

'Oh. Yes...' She looked at me and then down at the wheelchair. Marjorie didn't move. 'How's her friend?'

'Fine,' I said. 'I think they sent each other to sleep.'

The nurse laughed, looked at some notes she was holding, said, 'Well, goodbye,' and hurried to an important case.

We wheeled Marjorie down the corridor that led to the lift. We met a cleaner who was shaking her head over some patches of straw. 'I've seen it all now,' she muttered. 'What a place.' She went to fetch a vacuum cleaner.

The lift was empty. The reception area was deserted, but I was glad to get outside where the night was dark and the stars and moon obscured by clouds.

'Stay here,' I said to Sadie. 'I'll fetch the car.'

Marjorie said, 'What's happening?' Her head lolled and the hat fell off. I picked it up and slapped it back on her head.

'He's getting the car,' said Sadie.

'Where is it?'

'Over there.'

'And you are...'

'Sadie.'

I ran to the car-park, underneath the blue and red trellissing that fenced the walkways. Landscaped shrubberies were lit by electric lamps in goldfish bowls. Through the hospital windows, I could see nurses bending over beds, and doctors huddled in offices. The boiler house hummed gently behind me, and steam rose into the air.

As I drove up to the reception, I could see a nurse hurrying down the stairs from the first floor wards.

Sadie hadn't seen her – she waved at me. I parked badly, jumped out, ran round and opened the door. We were lifting Marjorie out of the wheelchair when the nurse ran past me and down to the car-park, where she was met by a man who kissed her and opened a car door for her.

Sadie was touched by my love for Marjorie. Marjorie mirrored the dead, fucked Dorset landscape. I drove slowly, as if the Alfa was a hearse. Say goodbye, barley corn and rock 'n' roll.

16

Marjorie and I had four visitors the next day. Clouds had gathered over the forest, and a few spots of rain blew against the windows. The cats were glad to be let in and fed. I fetched some logs, and was piling them up by the Rayburn when the first visitor arrived.

It was Dr Thubron. He'd come as soon as his surgery was finished. He was wearing odd socks. I took him upstairs, and we stood at the foot of Marjorie's bed.

'That stunt', he said to me, 'could have landed you in a lot of trouble.'

'Not while I'm alive,' she said. I had sat her up in bed, given her some juice and a light breakfast, but she wasn't as incapable as she looked or felt.

'You'd be much better off in hospital,' Thubron said.

'Why? How?'

He couldn't answer that.

'Show the doctor out, would you, Gregory?'

'OK.'

Downstairs, he held his arms up in mock surrender and said, 'I give in.' I opened the front door for him. 'But for God's sake call if you have to.' He fished in his bag and gave me a bottle of pills. 'These might help,' he said, and tried to describe what I knew to expect. I mentioned my parents. He mumbled about peas in a pod and left to attend a pregnant woman in Lyme.

*

I went for a walk in the forest because the second visitor arrived. He was Mr Kelman, a solicitor from Lyme. He had a grave face, a briefcase, a Saab 900, ginger hair, a dark pin-striped suit and black lace-up shoes with tiny, superficial spots punched into the toes. He introduced himself to me, and when Marjorie told me to go for a walk I did as I was told because half dead she was more alive than anyone else I knew. 'Get out and get some fresh air!' she groaned. 'Shake up your kidneys.'

It had begun to drizzle, but it was dry under the trees. Some primroses were growing on a bank between the edge of the wood and the fields below. Through the branches I could see a few sheep and the drizzle as it blew in curtains across the sky. The wind rustled the tree tops, but the wet silenced the birds. I tried to walk as softly as I could. I took slow, deliberate steps, rolling my feet on to the ground from heel to toe like a Red Indian.

Red Indians had an ancient and deliberate way of looking at nature. They never treated animals as 'game', or cut down trees unnecessarily. I tried not to stick out like a sore thumb, and followed a track through a plantation of sitkas until I reached a spinney of hazel that dipped into a hollow. This place had been a quarry once, but was disused and overgrown now. I sat down to eat some sandwiches and drink a can of beer.

I sat with my back to a bramble thicket; in my fatigues I blended well. After a while, the forest was weighed with enough water to start dripping. The beer was warm and the sandwiches cheese and tomato. I ate slowly. I had a mouthful when a deer walked into the hollow below me, sniffed the air and began to graze.

At first I thought it must have escaped from a zoo. Then I sat absolutely still and watched.

It heard something: it froze, tilted its head towards the noise but then went back to the grass.

It was a beautiful caramel-brown animal with a head like a greyhound's. Its ears seemed close enough to touch. They looked like little pockets. It had a stubby tail that stuck straight up, and perfect legs. Bambi.

Bambi was about thirty feet away. My mouth was full of cheese and tomato sandwich. The drips of rain came faster, and I felt myself about to gag. I slowly moved my hand to my mouth, and had got most of the bread out when I couldn't stop myself coughing – Bambi looked at me for a second before bolting for cover. His eyes were full of fear. I didn't mean to scare him. However hard I looked, I never saw Bambi again.

Colonel Franklyn was our third visitor. He sat in the kitchen with a far-away look in his eyes and said, 'I'm proud of you!' He clapped my knee. 'Initiative,' he said. 'That's the spirit! If more people were like you I don't think we'd be in such a mess.'

'I don't know about that,' I said.

'And modesty!'

Marjorie laughed. The Colonel fished in his pocket for his pipe, tapped it, topped it up, lit it and filled the room with clouds of acrid smoke that collected in shrouds that hung a foot above the floor. I thought about saying something about smoke following him like sheep, but Marjorie said, 'Yes. He's a very good boy,' as if I wasn't there, so I didn't bother.

The Colonel began to talk about D-Day. I sat and listened for a few minutes. He'd been involved in undercover operations. When he asked Marjorie if she remembered anything from those times, she nodded but didn't say anything.

*

Our fourth visitor arrived in the evening. After a short sleep and some fresh orange juice, Marjorie felt well enough to get up and sit in the kitchen. She had two of the cats on her lap. I was reading to her – 'A Psychological Experiment', a short story by Richard Marsh (1847–1915). I had her on the edge of her seat –

> The stranger dashed the knife he held into his own breast, or he seemed to. He cut the oilskin open from top to bottom. And there gushed forth, not his heart's blood, but an amazing mass of hissing, struggling, twisting serpents. They fell, all sorts and sizes, in a confused, furious, frenzied heap, upon the floor. In a moment the room seemed to be alive with snakes. They dashed hither and thither, in and out, round and round, in search either of refuge or revenge. And, as the snakes came on, the efts, the newts, the lizards, and the other creeping things, in their desire to escape them, crawled up the curtains, and the doors, and the walls.
>
> Mr Howitt gave utterance to a sort of strangled exclamation . . .

Someone knocked on the door.
'Good God,' Marjorie said. 'Who's that?'
'Shall I get it?'
'If you have to.' She huffed. 'But there'd better be a reason.'
It was Nicky. As soon as I let the door off the latch, he pushed it open and burst into the lodge, yelling, 'You won't get away with it! You won't! You'll regret ever coming down here.' He put his hand out to push me, but I backed off.
'What are you on about?' I said.

'You know what!' He pointed at me. His face was red. His hair was untidy.

'I'm trying to think,' I said, mockingly.

'Sadie! That's what!' he shouted. 'We had a date last night; now I hear she was off with you on some wild goose chase!'

'So what?'

'So—'

'She's free to do as she pleases, isn't she? It was an emergency, I asked her, she—'

'She's mine,' he whined.

'Oh, yeah? Like that heap you've got parked out there?'

'That heap could run your old bat's car off the road any day,' he said.

'Old bat?' I said. 'Who are you talking about?' I moved towards him. He stood his ground.

'You know.' He grinned. 'Why? What's the matter?'

'You're the matter.'

'Big talk.' He took a deep breath and expanded his chest. He bent towards me. 'I haven't heard,' he said.

'What?' I said.

'Is she dead yet?'

'No,' said Marjorie. She appeared from the kitchen and pointed her shotgun at Nicky. 'The old bat's not.' The gun waved about, but she was steady on her feet. The butt was crooked under her good arm, with a good finger on the trigger. I moved towards her. She pointed a bad finger at me. 'Stay there,' she said.

I didn't move.

She reminded me of the climactic scene in *True Grit*. John Wayne, with one (cancerous) lung, gallops across a plain with a rifle under each arm, shooting the bastards. Marjorie was wearing a nightie, dressing gown, socks and lambswool slippers.

Nicky froze. The colour drained from his face and

I noticed a slight dip develop in his knees, like he had lost three inches in height.

Marjorie dealt with him very quickly. She said, 'I'm going to be a dead old bat in a week's time, so life for shooting you wouldn't mean very much, would it?'

Nicky shook his head.

'And my reflexes aren't what they used to be. Gregory will tell you that.' I nodded. 'My fingers'll just start twitching for no reason at all. At any time at all.' She smiled. 'A moment's notice.' I nodded again.

'Oh.'

'So maybe you should leave . . . '

Nicky backed off.

' . . . and not come back. We were enjoying a very exciting story until you turned up. What was it called, Gregory?' She turned towards me, but kept the gun on Nicky. She was expert with it.

' "A Psychological Experiment",' I said.

Marjorie laughed. 'Maybe we could perform one on you.'

'A what?'

'A psychological experiment,' she said.

I was expressionless.

Nicky fumbled for the door handle.

I moved towards him and opened it. I could see his Capri parked at the bottom of the drive. The forest was rustling, but I couldn't see beyond the first two ranks of trees.

'I—' he said.

'I know,' said Marjorie.

His mouth dropped open.

'And don't try threatening my friend again,' Marjorie said. 'He's a desperate man.'

Nicky nodded, winced, looked at me and then back at Marjorie. I held the door wide open.

'Because if you do I'll have to put a curse on

you. Maybe I'll do that anyway.' She grinned, madly. 'You've heard of my powers? They're not lies.'

Nicky's eyes narrowed. He was caught between belief and being mocked, and wasn't used to the feeling. He nodded again.

'Good,' said Marjorie.

I smiled.

Nicky backed out of the door and across the gravel, until he disappeared into the gloom. I closed the door.

Marjorie was standing in the kitchen with the gun pointing at the ceiling. She smiled and pulled the trigger. The hammer clicked against the empty chamber. I made a cup of tea and finished reading 'A Psychological Experiment' to her.

As the stranger put them from him, Mr Howitt's head fell, face foremost, on to the table. His partner, lifting it up, gazed down at him.

Had the creature actually been what it was intended to represent it could not have worked more summary execution. The look which was on the dead man's face as his partner turned it upwards was terrible to see.

When I closed the book, Marjorie clapped her hands and said, 'Marvellous! A bit dated, but still marvellous!'

17

A month before Mum died, she said, 'I want to talk to you about Bruce.' The dog had just eaten a light supper of diced liver and was resting at her feet.

'What about him?' I said.

'What's going to happen to him when I'm gone?'

'I don't know; we'll sort something out.'

I put an advert in the paper.

> FREE TO GOOD HOME
> Well-behaved Bull Terrier dog

The enquiries taught me a few things about human nature. We had some calls from people who insulted me. 'A dog's for life, not just for Christmas' was the idea.

One evening I answered the phone, and before I got the chance to say anything a woman's voice screamed, *'If you can't look after the poor animal it's you who should be put down, not him!'*

'We're not talking about putting him down,' I said.

'But you would if nobody gives him a home! Do you know how many dogs the RSPCA puts down every week?'

'No.'

The woman told me.

I was impressed. I said, 'Do you know how many people die of cancer every week?'

'What's that got to do with it?'

I told her. I explained why we were looking for a good home for Bruce. I stressed the 'good'. There was silence on the other end of the line.

I asked the woman if she'd like to leave her number, so I could phone her and upset her. She didn't say anything, so I said, 'Fuck you,' and hung up.

Eventually, I found Bruce a good home, and though he had to put up with tinned food and bowls of water, the head of the household was a keen gardener. She had an allotment up the road and used to wheelbarrow her tools up there every other day. Bruce would trot alongside, barking at the barrow's wheel, and at the allotment would guard the tools and dream about diced liver.

One morning Marjorie said, 'I want to talk about the cats.' She was lying on the kitchen sofa with a glass of whisky on her lap. It was raining.

'What about them?' I was washing up.

'What's going to happen to them when I'm dead?'

'I don't know. Maybe Sadie would have them.'

'That's a good idea,' she said, and stroked the nearest.

I scrubbed a saucepan. 'Marjorie?'

'Yes?'

'Are you afraid of dying?'

'If you don't know the answer to that one by now,' she said, 'you're not a very observant boy.'

'I'm not a boy,' I said.

'How old are you?

I reminded her.

'You're a boy,' she said, 'and you'll go on being one if you keep asking questions like that.' She laughed, finished her whisky and asked me to pour another.

*

I went to a lot of trouble and spent enough money to sleep with Sadie in comfort. Asking her about having the cats was a footnote to the trouble. I booked a room in a bed and breakfast house in Lyme. There was a view of the harbour from the window, and stiff towels in the *en suite* bathroom.

I was full of lies. I told the woman in charge that we were on holiday, maybe even looking for a holiday cottage. I don't think she believed me, but I paid in advance, in cash. It was midday. We had one bag between us. I'd told Marjorie I was shopping in Axminster. Sadie told her father she would be back for milking. I closed the curtains. I could hear other people in the house, cleaning bathrooms and changing sheets.

As we were taking our clothes off, I said, 'Marjorie is very worried about her cats.'

'What's the matter with them?'

I hung my trousers over the end of the bed. 'It's not them. She's worried that they won't have anywhere to live when she's dead.'

'We'll have them,' she said.

I unhooked her bra. 'You're beautiful,' I said.

'You're not bad yourself.' She took her socks off, rolled them into a ball and threw them in my face. I punched them away, like Gordon Banks.

Her skin looked and felt like quality writing paper. Mine looked like bald chicken flesh. She nipped my ears. I reached down and pinched her behind her knees and we fell on to the bed.

I had a condom. I said, 'They were Hoovering them in the chemist's.'

'What?'

'The condoms. I laughed at the woman – she thought it was funny too, but said, "We're very clean here."'

I'd left a crack in the curtains, and the window was open. I could hear the waves crashing along the shore, and they got louder and louder as we made love.

The bed squeaked and boinged. We shifted into a dozen different positions. Each was shadowed by a different noise. When we didn't move we could hear someone polishing a sink in another room. We laughed.

'Have you ever done it in the rain?' I said, at one point. She looked over her shoulder and said, 'No. Have you?'
 'No.'
 'Let's!'
 'OK.'
 'When?'
 'Tomorrow?'
 'How?'
 'Hey!'
 'What?'
 'Do that again!'
 'What?'
 'What you did just then.'
 'This?'
 'Yeah! How do you do that?'
 'I don't know. You want it again?'
 'Go on, then . . .'
A slight breeze blew the curtains in.
The plumbing in the house was old.
The room smelt of old Brillo pads.
The sheets were stiff.
When we left, we had to walk through the kitchen.
The people that owned the place were having a cup of tea. They had the radio on, and were listening to a play about a chocolate manufacturer. There'd been a fire at the factory, but it hadn't done

serious damage. The radio was one of those old ones, with a huge illuminated dial.

'How's the room?' the woman said.

'Fine,' I said. Sadie was giggling behind me. 'Lovely view.'

'Isn't it?'

'Sorry?'

'Isn't it a lovely view?'

'Yes,' I said. 'I said it was.'

'I know.'

'But you asked if—' Sadie tugged my arm.

'Come on,' she said. 'I'd love to walk round the harbour.'

'Cobb,' said the woman.

'What?' I said.

'It's the Cobb.'

I felt light-headed, and ready for anything. I didn't argue. I said, 'OK,' and followed Sadie out.

We walked around the harbour. There weren't many boats in the water, but some fishermen were being picturesque with nets. One of them told us to 'Bloody watch it!'

The harbour walls were built in the 1820s by a gang of masons under the command of Captain William Fanshawe (Royal Engineers). I thought that the walls didn't have to be so beautiful and could have been more practical, but they were as practical as they needed to be, and more beautiful than they needed to be. There were subtle curves and angles, dips and rises, and a worn, leaning flight of steps to the top.

I said, 'Do you want to go up?'

Sadie said, 'Again?'

I said, 'Come on.'

'Already?' she said.

I waited for her at the end.

When she joined me, she said, 'It's like a big chop, isn't it?'

The air was fresh and salty; the coast, as it ran east to Portland, was obscured by low cloud. I cupped one of Sadie's buttocks in my hand – she put a hand over mine and squeezed. A fishing boat came into the harbour with gulls over its masts. The sea was running in deep, long swells.

'Lyme's always made me feel randy,' Sadie said. When a strong gust of wind almost blew us off our feet, she leant into it and swept her hair away from her face with a quick, easy action. 'Don't ask me why . . . '

'I wasn't going to.'

From where we stood, the town looked like part of fairyland. The sun was going down, and a few lights came on. Clouds hung in ribbons across the dimming light, and all the time the sea washed up and back below us.

'Isn't it beautiful?' she said.

'Yes.' I didn't look at her. 'Like you,' I said.

'And you.'

'You, you, you and you!' I yelled, but the wind and the sea stole my words.

As we walked back to the car, we held hands and talked about Marjorie's cats, fishing, and the generous proportions of some of the houses we passed. I could feel an unusual surging in my body, like snow was falling in my stomach. Sadie didn't have long legs. Her eyes were green and she had a little mole inside her right thigh.

18

On Tuesday, 7 March, Marjorie gave me instructions as usual. The most important job was to hoe the garden. The beans were showing. Also, I had to tidy the greenhouse and chop more logs.

There were enough logs to keep her going, but she said, again, 'You can't have enough logs.'

I didn't argue.

I fetched the tools. A flock of seagulls had flown inland to irritate a rookery on the edge of the forest. The rooks put up a loud show with their caws, and flew sorties against the intruders.

I was hoeing when a car drove slowly up the drive, parked in front of the lodge, and a smart couple climbed out. They were both carrying briefcases. He was wearing a brown suit, she was wearing a skirt, jacket and a hat.

I propped the hoe against the wheelbarrow, wiped my hands on my trousers and went over. They approached me, smiling.

'Good morning,' the man said.

'Can I help you?'

He opened his hands as if in blessing. 'Isn't it a beautiful day?' he said.

I nodded. 'What do you want?'

The woman smiled at the man and said, 'Did you know that the love of God is everywhere, and—'

'The love of God?' I said.

'Yes.'

'Why?'

'Why?'

'Yes,' I said. 'Why?'

'It's—' the man began.

'Are you Jehovah's Witnesses?' I said.

'We're all witness to—' the man said.

'We're Orthodox Jews,' I said. I knew this statement sent Jehovah's Witnesses packing.

'Praise the Lord!' cried the woman. 'Our faiths have so much in common!'

I had a busy day in front of me. I held up my hands, palms to the front and said, 'We've got nothing in common,' and I started to walk back to the garden.

The Witnesses didn't move. They stood where they were – I felt their eyes in my back as I picked up the hoe. I heard an upstairs window open. Marjorie stuck her head out and shouted, 'You heard him! Clear off already!'

They didn't argue. Her gaunt face and streaming white hair could have been plucked from hell or beyond, where Witness was denied and dead men walked. 'Clear off!' They drove a Morris 1300, a horrible car with a transverse engine you couldn't work on, and a body that rusted if you spat on it.

I went back to work and remembered shopping in Camden Town when a hippie tried to sell me a record of music recorded by people with a guru. My mother had just died. I was having trouble adjusting to the loss, and in an angry mood.

The hippie claimed to have found peace, and said that freaked-out Peter Green, 'finest British-born blues guitarist', played on the record. 'But he's not freaked out any more.'

I freaked. 'He freaked because people like you led him up the garden path!' I yelled.

'The garden path', said the hippie, 'is a very real place to be.'

I gave him one more chance. 'And what are you doing? Giving them away?' I pointed to the records.

'No, man. They're five pounds fifty.'

'Five fifty?'

'They're good sounds.'

I hit the hippie, and as he went down, kicked the records out of his hands and into the road where they were damaged by traffic. I laughed when the hippie tried to get his own back by biting my leg – I chopped him down.'Stitch that!' I yelled, and stalked off.

Mum died when she'd finished telling me her life story, with Bruce on her bed. He felt the moment she died. I'd gone down to make a cup of tea – the kettle was coming to the boil when he started whining. At first I thought the noise was in the water pipes, but then I heard him scratching at Mum's bedroom door.

I went up and he bolted past me when I opened the door – Mum was in bed with a surprised expression on her face. She'd never had a visit from a pools representative, but death must have felt like that to her. I closed her eyes, straightened the bedcovers, phoned the doctor and let Bruce into the garden, where he howled at the fence until next-door complained.

I was chopping wood by the store shed when I heard a gunshot from the lodge. At first I thought it had come from the woods, but when the echo cracked in front and behind me, and a pane in Marjorie's bedroom window shattered and glass rained down on the path that led to the vegetable garden, I put the axe down and chased into the house.

Time slowed down, but I didn't let it hold me back. I kicked my boots off, scared two cats away from the Rayburn and knocked a chair over. It was too hot in the kitchen, and I hadn't washed the breakfast things.

I never imagined that Marjorie would commit suicide. Even when I saw the gun for the first time, it didn't occur to me that she might use it on herself. She wasn't mentally ill. I believed her like I believed everything she said about nature.

The previous evening, I'd told her that Sadie was happy to have the cats. When she said, 'You could do a lot worse than that girl,' I believed her. When she pointed at the shotgun and said, 'The garden needs protection,' I believed her. When she'd said, 'Maybe you should leave and not come back,' to Nicky, he had believed her.

In times of crisis, it's easy to notice things you hadn't noticed before. I bolted across the hall and up the stairs – I noticed a picture on the wall by the stairs window. It was of a naked woman sitting on a chair, drying herself. The woman had her back to us; one arm was resting on the chair back while the other used a towel on her hair. The colours were white, orange and brown. Underneath, someone had written *Woman Drying Herself*, Degas (1834–1917). I took all this in in a moment, and then, in one bound, was standing outside Marjorie's bedroom.

I put my ear to the door. It was painted white. I couldn't hear anything. I felt a line of sweat on my top lip; I wiped it away before I put my hand on the knob, took a deep breath, turned it and walked in, blinking.

'Don't you knock before entering a woman's bedroom?' Marjorie said. She was sitting on a chair by the window, with the gun resting on the sill.

'I heard a shot!'

'I told you, didn't I? As soon as the beans are up those bloody jackdaws are down.'

'*Jackdaws*? I didn't see any!'

She laughed. 'That's because I frightened them off!'

'You frightened me.' I pointed to the window. 'And you broke the window.'

She looked at it and then at the gun. She nodded. 'I forgot. It kicks like a mule.'

'Marjorie?' I said.

'Yes?' She steadied the gun and crouched to sight along its barrel.

'Be careful.'

'Ha!'

'Don't laugh.'

'What do you expect? Be careful!' She shook her head. 'I could shoot before I could walk. My father—' There was a knock on the door downstairs.

It was Sadie. She had been running. 'I was in the woods! I heard a shot . . .'

'Come in,' I said, and when we were sitting in the kitchen, I explained. She thought it was funny.

'Why does everyone think it's funny?' I said.

'It's not really,' she said, but laughed again.

'I was expecting to have to scrape her off the ceiling!'

Sadie leant towards me, stroked the side of my face and kissed my lips as Marjorie shouted, 'Who is it?' down the stairs.

'Sadie!'

'Bring her up!'

We went upstairs. The three of us sat in the bedroom with the window open and the shotgun resting on the sill. Sadie had some twigs in her hair – I reached over and picked them out.

Four

19

I did not expect to be affected by spring, but my thoughts turned as flowers appeared in the hedges and sheltered hollows in the forest. I didn't mean to think about Sadie, or worry so much about Marjorie. I was there to muck in but my heart began to drip for them. I felt it at work in my chest, speeding up and reminding my brain. I tried to stop it by drinking, but that only clotted the drips, so they hung inside, swinging when I moved. When I held my hands out I couldn't stop my fingers shaking. I couldn't concentrate on anything for longer than a minute without either one face or the other floating by. Sometimes they came together, but didn't look at each other, only me. Their lips moved, but I couldn't hear what they said. I might be chopping logs, digging, mending a fence or washing up.

Sadie had soft lips, but didn't look athletic. She'd been closed and sad when I first saw her. I saw her come out of her shell – the more I saw her the further she came, and the more beautiful. I came to her by accident, and to love her as my heart ordered. I didn't resist. I had never argued with it before. It had never given an inch or me a chance. It's an old story.

Sadie had soft lips, but you don't have to know how soft. She said, 'I know what you're thinking.'

I said, 'How?'

We were walking along a track that ran beneath

some beech trees, dipped towards a cattle trough and then up Conegar Hill. The Colonel had told me that the last ravens in Dorset bred on Conegar Hill. I said, 'How?'

Sadie said, 'I can see it in your eyes.'

'What am I thinking?' I said.

I had been thinking about Marjorie. She was fading fast. She wanted to enjoy the sun but asked to have the curtains closed during the day. The light hurt her eyes, she said, sighing. The Colonel had come to play cards, but she wasn't strong enough to hold a hand, so he had sat by her bed and read a story about headless men and women stalking each other. She was losing her will, but tried to concentrate.

'You're thinking about Marjorie,' Sadie said.

I nodded.

Sadie had pale skin, it suited her. She'd washed her hair the night before and it blew in long brown screws around her face. Her lips were almost not pink. Wild snowdrops, primroses and daffodils grew in the hedges and spread over the fields.

'I never met anyone like her,' I said. 'She doesn't want to let go. I know she's in agony, but she only complains if I fuss over her. She doesn't complain about the pain. Sometimes I think she might be a witch. Not a bad one, though.'

'A white witch . . .' Sadie said.

'She's got some power, but it's not enough.'

'I wish I'd known her before.' She shook her head. 'You're stupid when you're a kid.'

'I don't know,' I said.

We crossed a tarmacked track and over a gate into a field. The path led to the top of the hill and a wood of beech, larches and Scots pine. 'I wish I'd known you before too,' she said.

I felt lucky.

When I was eight I felt lucky to have Dad. I never knew that I was the most important person in his life, but I'm glad I didn't. I didn't want to grow up to disappoint him.

When I was eight, he bought two tickets to the FA Cup Final. It wasn't a cold day, but Mum made me wear long johns. I wore one of Dad's scarves. Before we left, we had some hot tea. Mum said she was going to put her feet up while we were gone.

West Ham were playing Preston North End. Dad bought some cocoa outside the ground, and we sat in the car-park to drink it. Some people were eating sandwiches and arguing about Bobby Moore's fitness (a cruel, false rumour).

Compared to Upton Park, Wembley Stadium was a revelation. Compared to the swelling pain I began to feel in my gut, a headache was nothing. When we finished the cocoa, we had our tickets clipped, and jostled and climbed through the dark, curved tunnels that led to our seats.

We passed a gents on the way. Dad asked me if I wanted a piss. I said, 'No,' casually. I didn't mind using a urinal when I was just wearing trousers and pants, but I wasn't showing men in there that I was wearing long johns. As we climbed the terrace to our seats, I got a stabbing in my groin – it made me wince. By the time Dad turned to look at me, I felt OK, and he looked OK – and when he looked OK I felt OK, because I loved him.

A band was playing hymns. I sat back, but then buckled in my seat, tears came to my eyes and Dad said, 'Are you OK?'

I nodded.

'Greg?'

'What?'

'What's the matter?' He leant over me and held my shoulders.

I took a deep breath.

I was determined to see us crush Preston. The pain went away. 'I'm OK,' I said. Dad took his hands away, and I stood up and yelled, 'Come on, Hammers!'

The pain came back with a vengeance as the ref blew the whistle to start the match. As I twisted in the seat tears shot into my eyes and blinded me. I screamed and slipped off the seat. I felt Dad scooping me up and carrying me away, down the terrace and back to the tunnels beneath the seats, where the noise of the crowd was hollow and frightening.

Then I was in a St John's Ambulance room where no one knew what the matter was. My belly was tight and swollen. Someone called for an ambulance. Dad carried me out. There was a big nurse called Gladys who held my hand and patted Dad's arm. She had to be careful where she sat, so she didn't overbalance the ambulance.

At the hospital, no one knew what was wrong with me. Doctors came and felt me, I had a blood sample taken, I was X-rayed and embarrassed. When I buckled with pain, the doctors stood back and observed me carefully and then whispered to each other. Dad kept a hand on me all the time. His face was white and his eyes shiny.

Eventually, someone decided that my gut had got twisted somehow. Dad asked if I could have something for the pain. A nurse fetched a pill, and then I was put in a quiet room where he held my hand while the doctors went to an office to discuss me. He didn't know what to do. The corners of his mouth quivered. We could hear the match on a radio somewhere above us, but no details.

There was five minutes to play when I felt something relax inside me and I asked to have a piss. Dad helped me off the bed and sat me on a toilet behind a curtain. I waited for a moment before pissing for about three minutes. The relief was unbelievable. My belly went down like a burst balloon and as I finished we heard a great roar from the radio, and a doctor came into the quiet room. Dad smiled, explained and said, 'I think he was embarrassed to take his long johns down in the gents.'

The doctor joked, 'I would be too!'

I looked at the doctor. I took Dad's hand and he led me out of the hospital. West Ham 3, Preston North End 2. Dad never said he didn't mind missing the only chance he ever had to see the Hammers win the FA Cup – maybe luck had nothing to do with it.

If luck has nothing to do with it, and 'romantic' means anything, I thought it was romantic on Conegar Hill, but Sadie didn't. As we approached the wood, she stopped suddenly as a loud, mocking laugh rang out of the pines. 'Hear that?' she said.

'What is it?'

'Ravens.'

We stood by a hedge and listened to them call. In the field below us, a woman in a raincoat was checking sheep. There was no telling, I thought, what would happen at any turn down any road. Across the valley behind and below us, a continuous stream of traffic wound its way along the A35. We were all killing the world, so I didn't blame anybody then. Put the blame on anyone and you put it on yourself. You can't do everything by yourself, so you can't do anything – like for us, there is no solution, only extinction.

One of the ravens left its perch and flew across the fields that folded away around us. It glided for a while, beat its wings once, twisted its tail and turned away. The Colonel said ravens had a sense of humour.

I could make letters out of the way some hedges crossed the fields – an E, an F, an H and an L.

20

Marjorie spent the last ten days of her life in pain I could see. I called Dr Thubron a couple of times, but he only repeated what he'd said before about hospital and left stronger pills. I recognised them. They were blue.

She struggled to keep a grip on her senses, but it was hard work. Once or twice she was strong enough to curse her body for letting her down, but most of the time she resigned herself to a dignified retreat. The Colonel agreed that this was a brave thing for the old girl to do, but didn't stay long. For once, he let his act slip, and became a frailer old man than I'd seen before. 'The only parties you end up going to are funerals,' he said. He sucked his pipe. It made bubbly sounds. 'It's not right, is it?'

'I don't know,' I said. I was cooking lentils. 'I don't know anything about it.'

He looked at me for a long time before saying, 'I like a man who owns up to not knowing something. You're honest.' He hissed air through his teeth. 'She did well.'

'All her life,' I said.

'Truer words . . .'

She ate soup, but nothing else. Her arm began to tingle madly, and when Dr Thubron visited, sat on her bed and said that this was a good sign, the arm was healing, she laughed a quiet, silvery cackle that hung in the air and made us smile. 'Good,' she whispered. 'I like a bit of good news.' Then she told him to get off her bed.

She couldn't write lists any more, but I knew what had to be done. Once, she said I was a good nurse. I'd propped her up with three pillows behind her; her hair was spread across them like frost, and her face had sunk, but behind it I could see her young. Years are cruel to women, I thought. Sadie had absolutely smooth, clear skin. By moonlight, her stomach was like a mirror, and her breasts were like oranges. Carrying bales and churns and moving calves across sheds had given her strong arms, but they weren't over-developed. When Marjorie whispered, 'I know what you're thinking,' I didn't argue. She couldn't resist, so I bent over and kissed her. She smelt of soap and candle wax. Before I left the room, I helped her have a crap, but she didn't want me for anything else.

In the forest, nothing seemed to move, though I could hear sounds all around me. Some were high, in the branches, and others were on the ground, close. I sat with my back to a tall larch tree. Its branches were covered in bright green new shoots. 'Larches are the only common coniferous trees that shed their needles in winter'.

You could live in the forest and if you were careful, no one would need to object, and you wouldn't need to worry. You could trap rabbits, work for people in exchange for vegetables and water, and charm someone into letting you borrow their bath. You could refuse to tell anyone anything about yourself, and become a mystery, or you could tell lies and become a lie.

In Roman times, the forest stretched from Charmouth

inland in every direction. It is difficult to imagine what that looked or felt like.

From a hill, the only sign of life would be two or three thin columns of smoke pluming out of an unbroken sea of trees; at Exeter and Dorchester there were forts the size of a large car-park. At Axmouth, an estuary provided anchorage for galleys, and facilities for sailors who didn't dare venture inland. One decent road bisected the forest; other lonely and dangerous tracks wound through the undergrowth and trees. Few people knew what was further than five miles away; those who did were magic. Only birds were safe, and took on mythic status, like Marjorie.

At Bettiscombe, 'Home of the Screaming Skull of Bettiscombe Manor', we had walked around a cold, dark church, and Marjorie had picked up a book about the place – *Bettiscombe*, by Michael Pinney.

Dr Anne Ross, the Celtic scholar and archaeologist, has put forward a suggestion that Haucombe, the oak wood of Marshwood Vale, may be the remaining trace of a great forgotten Celtic, Druidic sacred forest, through which *a known Celtic treasure* was brought from Europe in Roman times . . .

She liked the idea of a known Celtic treasure being carried through the forest. Was it wrapped in sacks to make it look ordinary, or paraded? Who was responsible for it? What was it? I didn't know, and didn't want to know. Knowing that there had been a known Celtic treasure was enough. After some thought she agreed with me, and said I could be quite intelligent.

On my own in Haucombe Wood, I got the feeling that I was being watched, but when I turned round there was nothing there. The larches grew like excuses for the trees that had grown there before. Each one was planted exactly the same distance from the next, and all were the same height. No undergrowth grew around their trunks – the forest floor was beige and springy. I thought I saw Bambi, but she was a shaft of sunlight lighting a clump of scrub beyond the larches, where the forest was less of a desert, and a hedge ran towards the fields.

The mechanics of looking after a dying old woman came easily to me, and Marjorie resigned herself to losing dignity when I lost my temper at her with 'Dignity doesn't mean anything! Everybody's got to shit! A baby doesn't think about dignity!'

She shifted in her bed.

I said, 'It enjoys it.'

She said, 'I don't.'

'You know what I mean,' I said, and wiped her face. We'd had soup for lunch. 'People make up the idea of dignity to give themselves something to cling to. Real dignity is not worrying about something like that.' I pointed to the bedpan.

'Bloody soup,' Marjorie mumbled, ignoring me. 'I hate it.' She gulped, tipped her head back and smiled. 'I want some roast beef. Something I've got to chew.'

'Marjorie?'

'Roast beef,' she whispered, as if it was a perfume.

Or, on another day, she insisted on being carried downstairs and outside. The sun was very bright. No clouds in the sky. I lent her my shades and set her up by the Alfa. She had the shotgun. She was going to shoot a jackdaw.

I couldn't persuade her that it wasn't a good idea. Most of the beans had been lopped already, but if she wasn't going to cheat death, she was going to deliver it (her idea). She used the car to hide behind, but didn't get anything.

21

On 30 March, Sadie called at the lodge. I'd promised to meet her after milking, but couldn't leave Marjorie. She was having trouble breathing, so I'd called Dr Thubron again. He said she had eight hours to live, gave her a shot of morphine and shook his head. He was good at that.

Sadie sat with me in the kitchen. She was wearing a blue and white cotton skirt, a white top and looked fragile to me. I wanted to get close to her but something held me back – an idea of what she would look like as an old woman, or the feeling that it was raining. The day was warm and sunny. I could hear birdsong. The cats were skittish. I hadn't done much work – I'd been drinking since lunchtime.

'How is she?'

'Asleep,' I said. 'I don't know if I'll . . . ' I couldn't finish what I was trying to say: I hung my head, and when Sadie put her hand on it I felt a charge from her, like a wish.

At half past nine in the evening, Marjorie began to tell me her life story. I'd been sitting with her since seven. She'd been asleep for most of that time, but when she woke up and demanded a whisky, and managed to sit up by herself, I listened as if the story would beg questions in the morning and get answers. When she started to speak, her voice was weak but it grew in strength, so for a few minutes I thought I was dreaming, but then I wasn't.

'When I was six I got an encyclopedia for my birthday. I remember it almost as if it's in front of me now. There were pictures of machines and plants, and rare animals, but the ones I liked best were of countries. Natives standing in the desert with sticks . . .

'All the photographs were in that brown sort of black and white. You know?'

I nodded.

'I used to look at the faces of people in Africa, Australia, the Pacific, and I'd wonder if they could see me! I used to think that when I was a little girl!'

'I used to wonder how televisions worked,' I said. 'I used to think the people had to live inside them.'

'I was never that stupid.' She didn't mean it.

'No,' I said. 'I bet you weren't.'

'Father was hard at work all day. War had broken out – he volunteered but they wouldn't have him. Everybody knew why except me. I never knew, but he got a contract to make army shirts. He made money from the war, and I think he hated that, but it didn't stop him. And I think he compensated for not fighting by working so hard. Maybe that made Mother drink. I don't know . . .

'We were living in Bristol, then, after the war, after I left school, I trained to be a nurse.' She laughed. 'That's funny now, isn't it?'

I didn't say anything.

'I moved to London – that's where I met Alice.' She licked her lips. 'It's a lovely name, isn't it? Alice . . . '

'Yes.'

'We were the new girls on the ward. We'd qualified on the same day, but in different places.' She fished under her pillow for a handkerchief, and dabbed at the corners of her eyes. 'It's funny how little things throw people together, isn't it? We were totally different, but the same. Do you know that? Have you ever felt that with someone?'

'No,' I said.

She managed a smile. 'She spent all her money on the Party, I spent mine in the cinema, or drinking. We argued half the time, but joked the other. "The terrible twins", we were. And it was wonderful, wonderful for a few years. I met your mother when she was six. I remember sitting on the floor, playing with her dolls.' Marjorie nodded at me. 'What do you think about that?'

'Amazing.'

'But it wasn't enough.' She cut herself dead, drank some whisky and said, 'Not playing with your mother – I didn't mean that. But I wanted some adventure. Those pictures in the encyclopedia had stayed with me. They haunted me, so I packed in the job and took a train to Bristol. I was expecting Father to forbid me to leave the country, but I was surprised. He wished me luck and gave me twenty pounds! Mother didn't care what I did, but he did. I think he wanted me to have something he never had.'

'My dad was the same,' I said.

'I went to Australia. I nursed in Sydney – it was tough, but that's what I wanted, I think. I bought a motorbike – you know about that ... '

'I wouldn't mind it again.'

'No time,' she said.

In 1939 she returned to England. She was thirty-two. Her mother was dead, and her father had retired to a cottage in Dorset, where he was writing a book about *shirts*. He had become quite eccentric, but was respected by the other people who lived in Birdsmoorgate. She was working at a naval hospital in Portsmouth, and visited him whenever she could.

She remembered the Second World War with affection as well as horror. Men without legs would apologise to her for the trouble they were causing. Blinded men would describe her features perfectly. 'There,' she said. She pointed to her dressing table. 'Top drawer. There's a photograph of me.'

She was in her uniform with looks that stunned me. 'Is that you?' I said.

'Gregory! What's the matter?'

I didn't tell her. I put the picture back. Little flecks of spit had appeared at the corners of her mouth. I was going to wipe them for her, but she stopped my hand. Her fingers were thin and the knuckles stood out like bolts. Her face was almost gone, and her hair was like fog; her eyes were pale and the blisters on them had grown. It was hard to see anything in her that was in the photograph, but her mouth still had the same edge to it – a lopsidedness that hovered somewhere between a smile and sadness. As she held my arm with one hand and wiped her mouth with the other, and then put the handkerchief down, I kissed her lips. She didn't flinch. I could feel her breath leaving her body and going into me, like a guest, or someone who occupies your heart.

'I went to Africa in '46/'47. I'd stayed with Father for a year after the war, helping him at the cottage – like you've been doing. He was very happy. The book was finished – nobody was interested in publishing it – but he'd taken up gardening. Vegetables mainly. He had a better plot than that one.' She gestured towards the window. 'And he walked a lot too. We walked over to this place then – I remember. It's funny, isn't it?'

I nodded.

'Have you ever been to Africa?'

'No.'

Marjorie looked away from me and stared at the night before telling me that I should go before it was

147

gone. 'They were very friendly to me,' she said. 'And keen to learn. Keen as mustard...'

'To learn what?'

'Anything. Anything – how to tie shoelaces, speak English, give injections, set a broken leg – anything. How to scramble eggs!'

In 1951, she was organising a malaria immunisation programme near Beni, Congo, on the Ugandan border. Her clinic was miles from the nearest decent road, surrounded on three sides by impenetrable jungle. She was explaining to some village elders about the importance of hygiene when a thin messenger came from Butembo with a letter for her. The elders were anxious to keep the stamp. King George the Sixth was known as a fair bloke. The letter was from Dorset. Marjorie's father was dying.

She left for England in the morning. The journey took two months – her father was dead and buried by the time she reached Birdsmoorgate, where she was greeted with a great deal of suspicion.

'I stayed six months before going back. I sold the old cottage – when I left I never thought I'd see England again. I was cutting all my ties. I hardly felt English any more – I don't know who I thought I was, only that I wanted to go home.' She laughed. 'Home?'

'Roots,' I said.

'What did you say?'

I shook my head. 'Roots. People look for their roots.'

'People look for a lot of things,' said Marjorie.

She went back to confusing native Africans with plasters and antiseptic creams. She suffered a year of regret – not knowing her father as well as she would have liked, not keeping up with Alice, wishing she'd found a sense of adventure in England – but this feeling passed, and she was left with herself. 'You have to find it in yourself,' she said.

'What's it?' I said.

'I can't tell you that. If you don't know what I mean – what's the use?' She smiled. 'But I think you're lying. You do know what I mean...'

True.

She stayed in Africa – Zaire, the Congo and Uganda – for twenty-six years. She found all the adventure she wanted – was lucky to escape with her life five times, was written into tribal folklore as the spirit of an invincible antelope, and she spread her message of hygiene over thousands of square miles. Her hair was bleached white by the sun, so she could be seen coming from miles away, as if a mirror was balanced on her head. She wore loose clothes and carried a bag that became known as an antelope's udder.

Then, in 1977, aged seventy, she woke up from a dream in which she'd smelt the fields that grew around the cottage in Birdsmoorgate, and realised that she had to see England before she died. 'I never thought I'd last this long,' she said. 'I thought I had three or four years. No more. Not twelve.'

'Why didn't you go back?'

She thought. 'I don't know. Maybe I was stupid. Maybe Alice...'

'What about Alice?'

'We were very close, before the war. I left – I was always guilty, or felt I was. She stayed and tried to make a better world. Or she thought she was making a better world. I went off and pleased myself.'

'You didn't!' I cried. 'You did more than Alice ever did! You made people well. You taught them...'

'That was just an excuse.'

'Marjorie!'

She looked at me. True. I shook my head.

She said, 'The M'Bochi respect the dying. Old people are venerated all over Africa. I never thought I'd become the local witch! You know, once I was stripped naked and painted head to foot in the colours of an Eagle God! I could fly to heaven!'

'You will,' I said.

'Maybe,' she said. 'Maybe there're people out there who'd have died without me.'

'Not maybe,' I said, but she didn't say anything else.

I went downstairs to make her a fresh hot water bottle. The cats were sitting around the Rayburn, and hassled me when I went to the fridge for some milk. I gave them some crunchy biscuits, but they looked scornfully at them, and then at me.

Marjorie never needed the hot water bottle. She had died with her eyes closed and a smile on her lips. I took two of the pillows away, and laid her flat on the bed. I straightened the covers and folded her good arm over the broken one before phoning Dr Thubron. When he came, he completed the death certificate, retrieved two bottles of pain killers and asked me if I was all right. I nodded, and said, 'Yes.'

22

Undertakers took Marjorie away in the morning, and in the afternoon Mr Kelman, the solicitor, phoned.

'Miss Calder was very specific,' he said. 'Maybe you could visit the office at your convenience.'

We arranged a date.

March 31 was a cold foggy day.

The cats knew she was dead.

Maybe some M'Bochi had picked up the scent, and were displaying mourning beads.

The forest was bastard dark, even in the middle of the day. I watched the trees from the kitchen window, but didn't go for a walk. I watched a few birds defend territory and build nests, and once, I saw a rabbit.

I lost interest in the vegetable garden, but still chopped logs (out of habit). I barrowed them to the shed and stacked them the way she'd shown me.

I moved a mattress into the kitchen.

Sadie called, but I put her off until after the funeral. I couldn't bear to look in her eyes because I wanted to dive into them and see myself as she saw me. I wanted to know what she felt, but couldn't say what I felt. She said, 'You look awful.'

'I feel it.'

'Do you need anything?'

I looked at her mouth. 'I'm all right.'

The day before the funeral, Alice arrived. I moved

the mattress out of the kitchen and went to meet her at Axminster station.

The train was late, but she didn't complain. She was very quiet in the car, but when we got to the lodge, she said, 'It's exactly as I remember it. Even the cats.' I hadn't taken them to Sadie's. The Rayburn was smoking – I hadn't been able to control it. When I got a flame going, it turned into clouds of smoke that belched out of the cracks between the hot plates, and out of the doors. I made a cup of tea, but the kettle took ages to boil.

Alice wanted to know what I was going to do.

'Go to the funeral,' I said.

'You know what I mean.'

'Do I?' I said angrily.

'Yes. You know exactly what I mean.'

I sipped my tea. It was disgusting, so I fetched a bottle of whisky. Alice didn't drink. It sapped her resolve.

'I'm going to...' I said, but couldn't say what I meant.

When Dad died, I cried. When Mum died, I felt totally alone and couldn't cry because – maybe – I had no one to hold. I drifted for too long. The quiet life was another lie: I bumped into Marjorie – her death made me angry. Alice understood that, told me not to stay up late and went to bed early.

I drove Alice and the Colonel to the funeral. He wasn't sure about riding in an Italian car. 'Took a hell of a beating in Sicily,' he mumbled. Alice chided him for this. I kept out of it, and drove respectfully.

The weather was good, birds flying, farmers driving tractors in shirtsleeves. I stopped for one to pass, but didn't look up. The roads were dry.

The Church of St Candida (St Wite) and Holy Cross,

Whitchurch Canonicorum, had a full visitors' book, a Norman inner porch door, a Perpendicular tower and is the only Anglican parish church in England that contains the enshrined relics of its patron saint.

St Wite lived in the Marshwood Vale when Coney's Castle watched and protected the area from Danish attack. Or she was the daughter of a Prince of Brittany who lost two fingers in a piratical axe attack and walked across the English Channel. Or she was a monk who went to Germany to evangelise the people. Whatever – she was martyred and her bones rest in a stone coffin set into the north wall of the church. Below the coffin, three oval holes allow injured limbs to be inserted for cure, or messages and posies to be left.

The vicar was sincere, and didn't preach.

As we stood around the grave and stared into the hole, an early butterfly, attracted by the coffin's brass fittings, fluttered down and rested on one of the handles. The weather was warm; the trees and bushes in the churchyard were budding with new shoots. Patches of primroses grew around some of the old tombs, and bluebells by the hedges. Some graves had fresh flowers in pots, others were neatly trimmed and laid with fresh gravel. When I looked up, I could see the crude carvings of a Viking axe and ship on the church tower – carved in haste, I thought. A dog barked for a few minutes, but it wasn't a bull terrier. It had a deeper note, an Alsatian, or a Labrador.

As we stood and paid last respects, some hikers came into the yard, admired the yew trees and sat beneath one to eat their sandwiches. I could see that they irritated the Colonel, but Marjorie would have thought they were a good touch. Sheep and lambs were grazing a field behind us. After a decent time, the vicar raised his head, and we took that as a sign, and left.

*

At the lodge, we opened a bottle of whisky and sat with the cats to drink it. I got drunk first, then the Colonel. Alice had one small glass, then made herself a cup of tea.

She fetched a book of old photographs and sat by the Rayburn, slowly leafing through them, occasionally lingering over one, putting her hand over it, tipping her head back and wiping the corners of her eyes.

'She was—' I tried to say.

'A champion!' the Colonel cried. 'A champion. I never met a woman like her.'

'Nor did I.'

'Boadicea!'

Alice turned a page and gave a little gasp.

'What've you found?' I said.

'Or someone like that . . . '

Alice turned the page quickly. 'Nothing. They're just old pictures. Old memories.'

'Memories,' the Colonel mumbled. 'It's all just memories. Photographs and memories. Not even telephone calls any more.' He looked at me. 'I've got a boy about your age. Lives in Hong Kong. It's always the middle of the night there.' He got his pipe out and started to fill it. 'A grandson I've never seen.' He scraped the pipe bowl without looking at it. 'He's one memory I could have now. Something for the future.' He laughed. I'd never heard him laugh before. It came from his throat, and shot from his mouth in a short, cutting snort, like a gun. 'Future! It's just bloody memories—' He turned and sat up. 'I'm sorry,' he said. 'Not in front of a lady. Apologies . . . '

'For what?' Alice looked up.

He shook his head. 'It doesn't matter,' he said.

Alice looked back at the photographs. 'No,' she said. 'It doesn't really.'

Five

23

I called on Sadie in the evening. It was still light. The fields were grey, but the sky was pink. Her mother held back two dogs when she answered the door. She asked me into the kitchen. Sadie's father was washing his hands.

'I was so sorry to hear about Marjorie,' she said. She put a bowl of milk down for the dogs.

'Yes,' he said, drying his hands. He was a friendly man. When he'd finished, he rolled his sleeves down, buttoned them, came over and shook my hand.

'No one really knew much about her. She kept herself to herself most of the time.'

'But she always had the time of day for us . . .'

I didn't say anything.

Sadie was washing down the milking parlour. When I went to see her, she stopped work to come over, put her arms around me and say, 'I'm sorry.' She traced a line down the side of my face with a finger. 'Are you OK?'

I nodded, but couldn't say anything. I'd gone past being drunk, into a place where the light was red, and nothing seemed to matter. The sound of her voice was like church music, and where she'd touched my face burned. I was steady on my feet, and capable in every way, but I still didn't say anything.

'Would you like to go for a drink?'

I shrugged.

She moved towards me and lightly kissed me on the cheek. 'I'll finish up,' she said.

I sat on a box and watched her. She was wearing jeans and short rubber boots. When she did the milking she wore a long green mac, but she'd taken it off to sweep the parlour. I stared, concentrating on her body, but when she looked up and smiled, she went out of focus, and my eyes filled with tears.

Sadie took me to a pub, sat me in a corner and bought the drinks. She held my hand but didn't say anything. I hadn't shaved, or washed my hair.

I was thinking about going to London or Bristol or Liverpool when she squeezed my hand, leant towards me and whispered, 'I love you,' in my ear. Her breath smelt of cake.

I turned to her and said, 'Thank you.' She tilted her head towards me and I kissed her on the lips.

She tasted sweet. I had put my tongue in her mouth when I felt a sharp tap on my shoulder. I broke away from Sadie, looked up and recognised Nicky, but I couldn't dodge his fist. He hit me on the chin. As I went down, I heard him yell, 'Where's the old bat now?'

I didn't feel any pain; as I fell, I twisted and grabbed his leg. He was wearing black trousers, white socks and white trainers. He was off balance, and tipped sideways, towards the table. As he smashed on to it, Sadie jumped up screaming, and dived for cover as glasses, ashtrays and coasters flew in all directions.

I got up, and was about to leap on Nicky when I noticed a fast motion out of the corner of my eye, and ducked. His friend Jack had tried to deck me with a chair. I picked one up myself and charged him, yelling like an elephant.

Other customers were cowering or diving for cover. Nicky was recovering. I pinned Jack against the bar, bared my teeth, growled, rolled my eyes and enjoyed the worried look in his eyes before I nutted him. When I took the chair away, he went down with a relieved expression on his face, and a little curl of blood on his forehead, like a question mark.

I stepped away from him and turned round in time to see Nicky approach with a beer mug in his hand. He waved it at me, leering. His jacket was torn, and some cigarette ash was smeared down the front of his trousers.

'I'm champion with one of these,' he said.

'A mug?' I said.

He nodded.

I heard someone laugh nervously.

I was still holding the chair. I said, 'Want a seat?' and waved it at him.

He slashed towards me.

I parried the attempt and lunged at his head.

He ducked and advanced.

I backed off, poking the chair at him.

He grinned, and rushed me, and smashed the mug against one of the legs. Shards of glass flew into the air. The crowd backed further away from us. I put an arm up to cover my face. As I did, Nicky kicked the chair out of the other and slashed again. I swerved, but this time he caught my cheek.

I didn't feel a thing. Some blood ran into my mouth and dripped on to the floor. As soon as I tasted it, something snapped in my head. A sudden hot blast burned in my ears and spread behind me and down my back. I yelled, *'Bastard!'* and charged him.

He hesitated. I slipped on some spilt beer – this was luck. As I went down, I found myself level with his knees. I grabbed them and pushed. I felt Nicky bend as he tried to slash me again, but before he could I had him over. I twisted away before he landed, and braced myself with a table leg. I heard a sickening crunch, and more glass smashing as I hauled myself to my feet.

I turned around as Nicky began to pick himself up. When he turned and I faced up to him again, I could see that he was having trouble focusing. He shook his head and rubbed it. Bubbles of blood were popping out of his nose. He moved towards me and stood on some glass. He looked down, lifted his right foot, looked at the bottom of his shoes and then looked at me, as if he wasn't sure who I was or where he was. I gave him a big smile, but didn't move towards him. He looked quizzically, but understood when Sadie smashed him over the back of the head with a pool cue. The light left his eyes so quickly that I didn't see it go, and then he was asleep.

The landlord moved out of the crowd, pointing his finger at me. 'Look—' he said.

'*No!*' I yelled. 'You look! You fucking look!' I was boiling with venom. Blood was pouring out of my cheek and nose and dripping on to the floor. Nicky was very still. Jack didn't move. I pointed out of the window and said, 'There was a woman living up the road here, and people like him—' I pointed at Nicky '—called her an old bat. People like him and the rest of you!' I knew my eyes looked dangerous, and my voice sounded mad.

There was some rustling amongst the other customers, but no one made a move.

'And you lot wouldn't know it if it bit your arses!' I took a deep, wheezing breath and fumbled for a handkerchief. I held it against my cheek. 'She was worth more than all of you put together, but you didn't know that, did you?'

No answer.

'She was just an old bat, wasn't she?' I laughed, madly. 'But now you're going to have to find someone to take her place.'

Some murmurings. I moved backwards, towards the door. 'It is, isn't it?' I said, grinning.

'What?' said the landlord.'

'Bow and arrow country.'

'What?'

I was almost at the door. 'You heard,' I said.

I looked around and saw Sadie. She was about eight feet away from me. She was still holding the pool cue, but didn't move.

I reached into my pocket and took out a handful of change. There was four or five pounds there. 'That's for the damage,' I said, and threw it into the crowd, and while everybody watched the coins fall and then scrabbled for them, I left. A moment later Sadie followed, and we drove back to the lodge.

24

I was sitting in Mr Kelman's waiting room with Alice. My face was cleaned up but had throbbed all day.

Mr Kelman's secretaries were trained to work efficiently in the presence of grieving relatives or hung-over beneficiaries. One of them was cursing her computer, but quietly. There was a pile of sailing magazines there, and advertisements for interest rates. We sat on chrome-framed chairs. No words were exchanged, apart from, 'We've got an appointment with Mr Kelman', and 'If you'd like to wait here, I'll tell him you're here', and 'Would you like to come this way?' when he was ready for us.

'As you may or may not know,' Mr Kelman began, 'Miss Calder died a—' he cleared his throat, ' — wealthy woman. Her accounts show that she was a regular and careful saver and in addition, of course, she was the original sole beneficiary of the late Mr Calder's estate.' He tapped a file. 'The shirt manufacturer . . . '

Alice nodded.

I looked blank.

'The shirt manufacturer,' Mr Kelman repeated. He picked up a rubber band, hooked it over a finger and stretched it before checking himself and putting it down again.

'Yes,' said Alice.

'So...' he continued, leaning back and rubbing under his right eye, 'we turn to the Will.' It was on the desk – he picked it up, undid a ribbon that was tied around it, and coiled this into a mug with a seagull and *Land's End* written on it. 'She revised it less than a week ago,' he said, 'in your favour, Mr Thompson.'

'In my favour?' I said.

'That is correct.'

'Why?'

Mr Kelman shook his head. 'That's not for me to say.' He lowered his voice, but I heard him say, 'Not that that's particularly unusual...'

'What?' I said.

'Mr Thompson?'

'What's not particularly unusual?'

He scratched his eyes. 'People often feel the need to change their minds at the last minute.'

'Maybe they see things more clearly then.'

'That's one way of looking at it,' Mr Kelman said, as if he was humouring me.

Alice didn't say anything.

I got five thousand pounds, the Alfa, and any three of Marjorie's possessions.

Mr Kelman read: ' "For helping with my dignity", she says,' he said, and then, after clearing his throat again, told Alice that the Communist Party of Great Britain was beneficiary of the bulk of the estate, 'a little under half a million, property included, of course. You're named as Trustee.'

'Me?' said Alice. 'Us?' She was on the edge of her seat, gripping her hands together.

'Yes.'

'My God.'

Mr Kelman was obviously appalled by this stipulation, but he was a professional, and used to coping under stress.

I said, 'I thought you were an atheist,' to Alice, but she didn't hear me.

Alice and I walked down the main street and along the front to the harbour. My hangover had cushioned the shock, but I still couldn't believe that I could drive out of Dorset in my own Alfa. Alice was dumbstruck. We sat on a bench and watched the sea roll in over the shingle.

'I never thought,' she said, 'Never imagined . . .'

'What?'

'She—'

'Alice?' I didn't wait for her to say anything. 'What was it between you two?'

She sat in silence for a while, before saying, 'Lots of things. Good times. Love, guilt . . .'

'Marjorie said she felt guilty about going off.'

'What else did she talk about?'

I shrugged. 'Her father. Australia. Africa.'

'It's strange,' Alice said. 'I felt guilty about making her feel guilty.'

'Why?'

She shook her head. 'Who knows? Who knows why these things start, but it's a downward spiral.' She stared at the sea and sighed. 'I suppose it's what happens to lovers,' she said, eventually. 'But we never had a chance.'

'What?' I said.

She didn't hear me. 'It was different in those days. People are more tolerant these days. They're not so kind, but they're more tolerant. We used to be unnatural – now we're just another minority.' She shook her head.

It was too rough for any fishing, but two men walked by with a pair of oars between them.

'I think I preferred it when I was unnatural. There're

too many minorities these days. Everybody's in a minority . . .'

'I'm not.'

She stopped musing and looked at me. 'Yes, you are. A minority of one.'

'You can't have a minority of one.'

'Yes, you can! You can have anything you want!' She took my hand and said, 'Do you know what your trouble is, Gregory?'

'No. What?'

'You don't want to control your own life. You believe in fate.'

'How do you know?'

'I know.' She nodded, meaningfully. 'And it's true, isn't it?' she said.

I nodded.

'Don't,' she said. 'Fate's just another god. It's something you can believe in. Don't believe in anything and then you'll understand. No method—'

'Communism is a method—'

'No, it's not. Not at all. It's just a means to an end.'

'What's the difference?'

She didn't answer.

A group of comprehensive school children walked by. They were carrying bottles of cider and laughing at something they'd seen on the beach. One of the girls was hanging on to two boys. Another boy hung back and leant against a lamp-post with another girl. Periods of bright sunshine were interrupted when slips of dark cloud scudded across the sky and blocked out the light. 'She didn't have to do that,' Alice said. 'Guilt's not worth that much,' but she didn't say anything else.

25

No one is ever satisfied with the weather they get, but the forest took what it got without complaint. When I couldn't sleep, I went for a walk in it. It was half past four in the morning – as I passed Alice's room I could hear her snoring.

I stood in the kitchen to put my boots on. The Rayburn had gone out, and I hadn't washed the dishes. Marjorie had always washed up as soon as a meal was finished.

I met one of the cats in the garden. It came up to me and rubbed against my leg when I stopped to look at where I'd planted the beans. There was nothing there.

The first faint streaks of light were showing on the eastern horizon, but in the forest it was as pitch black as midnight, and solid, like a door.

A strong wind blew through the trees, and though they protected me from the worst of it, the top branches thrashed and beat against each other. The noise was frightening but I wasn't spooked, and didn't want to go back to the lodge. I could see the hall light shining through the glass in the front door, but when I climbed a rise in the forest and then took a track that led down towards Bambi's hollow, I couldn't see it any more.

I didn't meet Bambi or anything else. No birds called – without them the trees seemed naked. A song came into my head, a melody. I tried to whistle it but I was dry. I didn't get any of the words.

Past Bambi's hollow, I walked through an overgrown area. It was difficult to see the way, but the path wasn't slippery. I crossed a wider track and climbed to a hedge that bordered the forest where I sat on a fallen trunk and watched the sun rise.

It came slowly, but the light changed quickly. The first birds started to sing as the colours in the forest began to show. The tree trunks were grey, and the outlines of the top branches gradually appeared, and the fields below me swam out of the darkness as if they'd slipped out of a cave, twinkling with frost.

Alice stayed on to sort out Marjorie's things. I took the cats to Sadie's. We sat in the kitchen and she poured two beers. Her parents were at market with five calves.

'I'll leave them in the laundry room for a couple of days,' she said, pointing to the cats. They looked straight at me, as if it was my fault.

'Three days?'

'They'll go back to the lodge if I don't.' She spoke with authority.

'OK,' I said. 'If you say so.'

We took our beer upstairs to her bedroom. She had photos of cows on her walls, and some rosettes. There was a dressing table by the window, with her hairbrush on it, and some dried flowers pushed into the corner of the mirror. We got undressed and into bed. Her bed was very narrow. I found a hot water bottle shaped like a bear in it. I lay on my back with my drink on my chest. Sadie lay on her side with her hand on my stomach and the other resting behind my head.

She said, 'What are you going to do?'

I shrugged.

She kissed my chest. 'Are you going to stay at the lodge?'

I drank some beer and said, 'I don't know. Sometimes I wish I was one of the cats.'

We listened to a cockerel crowing in the yard. From the window I could see the edge of the forest. 'You could get a job round here,' she said.

A pair of crows flew out of the forest and flapped lazily towards the fields below. 'I could get a job anywhere,' I said. I looked down at her. She looked away and blinked before closing her eyes and resting her head on my shoulder.

*This novel is for
Neil Reid
and
Caroline Chivers*

FOR THE BEST IN PAPERBACKS, LOOK FOR THE 🐧

In every corner of the world, on every subject under the sun, Penguin represents quality and variety – the very best in publishing today.

For complete information about books available from Penguin – including Puffins, Penguin Classics and Arkana – and how to order them, write to us at the appropriate address below. Please note that for copyright reasons the selection of books varies from country to country.

In the United Kingdom: Please write to *Dept E.P., Penguin Books Ltd, Harmondsworth, Middlesex, UB7 0DA.*

If you have any difficulty in obtaining a title, please send your order with the correct money, plus ten per cent for postage and packaging, to *PO Box No 11, West Drayton, Middlesex*

In the United States: Please write to *Dept BA, Penguin, 299 Murray Hill Parkway, East Rutherford, New Jersey 07073*

In Canada: Please write to *Penguin Books Canada Ltd, 2801 John Street, Markham, Ontario L3R 1B4*

In Australia: Please write to the *Marketing Department, Penguin Books Australia Ltd, P.O. Box 257, Ringwood, Victoria 3134*

In New Zealand: Please write to the *Marketing Department, Penguin Books (NZ) Ltd, Private Bag, Takapuna, Auckland 9*

In India: Please write to *Penguin Overseas Ltd, 706 Eros Apartments, 56 Nehru Place, New Delhi, 110019*

In the Netherlands: Please write to *Penguin Books Netherlands B.V., Postbus 195, NL-1380AD Weesp*

In West Germany: Please write to *Penguin Books Ltd, Friedrichstrasse 10–12, D–6000 Frankfurt/Main 1*

In Spain: Please write to *Longman Penguin España, Calle San Nicolas 15, E–28013 Madrid*

In Italy: Please write to *Penguin Italia s.r.l., Via Como 4, I-20096 Pioltello (Milano)*

In France: Please write to *Penguin Books Ltd, 39 Rue de Montmorency, F-75003 Paris*

In Japan: Please write to *Longman Penguin Japan Co Ltd, Yamaguchi Building, 2–12–9 Kanda Jimbocho, Chiyoda-Ku, Tokyo 101*

BY THE SAME AUTHOR

A Lesser Dependency

'On a night in September 1971, Maude, Leonard, Odette and all the remaining Ilois left Diego Garcia forever ...'

'Peter Benson, through the experiences of this one family, shows how heaven turned to hell ... This account of a shocking, shaming business smoulders with quiet anger' – *Time Out*

'It tells of the fate of a family of Ilois natives who are driven from their Indian Ocean paradise of Diego Garcia when the island is handed over to the American military. The patient nobility of the central characters, as they slide from contentment to poverty and death, is never in question' – *Daily Telegraph*

'Their world is established with authority; there's a sense of sun and time and a way of life that has gone on unchanged for centuries ... A powerful political novel which makes its case all the more forcefully for being so restrained' – *Guardian*

and, winner of the Guardian *Fiction Prize:*

The Levels

Set in the secret landscape of the Somerset Levels, Peter Benson's remarkable first novel is the story of a young boy whose first encounter with love both bruises and enlarges his vision of the world.

'It discovers things about life that we recognise with a gasp' – *The Times*